Morrigan in the Sunglare
SETH DICKINSON

Things Laporte says, during the war—

The big thing, at the end:
The navigators tell Laporte that *Indus* is falling into the sun.
Think about the *difficulty* of it. On Earth, Mars, the moons of Jupiter, the sun wants you but it cannot have you: you slip sideways fast enough to miss. This is the truth of orbit, a hand-me-down birthright of velocity between your world and the fire. You never think about it.

Unless you want to fall. Then you need to strip all that speed away. Navigators call it *killing your velocity* (killing again: Laporte's not sure whether this is any kind of funny). It takes more thrust to fall into the sun than to escape out to the stars.

Indus made a blind jump, fleeing the carnage, exit velocity uncertain. And here they are. Falling.

They are the last of *Indus'* pilots and there is nothing left to fly, so Laporte and Simms sit in the empty briefing room and play caps. The ship groans around them, ruined hull protesting the efforts of the damage control crews—racing to revive engines and jump drive before CME radiation sleets through tattered armor and kills everyone on board.

"What do you think our dosage is?" Laporte asks.

"I don't know. Left my badge in my bunk." Simms rakes her sweat-soaked hair, selects a cap, and antes. Red emergency light on her collarbone, on the delta of muscle there. "Saw a whole damage control party asleep in the number two causeway. Radiation fatigue."

"So fast? That's bad, boss." Laporte watches her Captain, pale lanky daughter of Marineris sprawled across three seats in the half-shed tangle of her flight suit, and makes a fearful search for damage. Radiation poisoning, or worse. A deeper sort of wound.

In the beginning Simms was broken and Laporte saved her, a truth Simms has never acknowledged but must *must* know. And she saved Laporte in turn, by ferocity, by hate, by being the avatar of everything Laporte didn't know.

And here in the sunglare Laporte is afraid that the saving's been undone. Not that it should matter, this concern of hearts, when they'll all be dead so soon—but—

"Hey," Laporte says, catching on. "You *sneak,* boss. I call bullshit."

"Got me." Simms pushes the bottlecap (ARD/AE-002 ANTI RADIATION, it says) across. A little tremble in her fingers. Not so severe. "They're all too busy to sleep."

The caps game is an Ubuntu game, a children's game, a kill-time game, an I'm-afraid game. Say something, truth or lie. See if your friends call it right.

It teaches you to see other people. Martin Mandho, during a childhood visit, told her that. *This is why it's so popular in the military. Discipline and killing require dehumanization. The caps game lets soldiers reclaim shared subjectivity.*

"Your go, Morrigan," Simms says, shuffling her pile of ARD/AE-002 caps. The callsign might be a habit, might be a reminder: *we're still soldiers.*

"I was in CIC. Think I saw Captain Sorensen tearing up over a picture of Captain Kyrematen." *Yangtze's* skipper, Sorensen's comrade. Lost.

Simms' face armors up. "I don't want to talk about anything that just happened."

"Is that a call?"

"No. Of course it's true."

Laporte wants to stand up and say: fuck this. Fuck this stupid game, fuck the rank insignia, fuck the rules. We're falling into the sun, there's no rescue coming. Boss, I—

But what would she say? It's not as simple as the obvious thing (and boy, it's obvious), not about lust or discipline or loyalty. Bigger than that, truer than that, full of guilt and fire and salvation, because what she really wants to say is something about—

About how Simms is—important, right, but that's not it. That's not big enough.

Laporte can't get her tongue around it. She doesn't know how to say it.

Simms closes her eyes for a moment. In the near distance, another radiation alarm joins the threnody.

Things Laporte already knows how to say—

I'm going to kill that one, yes, I killed him. Say it like this:

CLARKESWORLD

MARCH 2014 - ISSUE 90

FICTION

NON-FICTION

Neil Clarke: Publisher/Editor-in-Chief
Sean Wallace: Editor
Kate Baker: Non-Fiction Editor/Podcast Director
Gardner Dozois: Reprint Editor

Clarkesworld Magazine (ISSN: 1937-7843) • Issue 90 • March 2014

© Clarkesworld Magazine, 2014
www.clarkesworldmagazine.com

Morrigan, tally bandit. Knife advantage, have pure, pressing now. Guns guns guns.

And the ship in her sights, silver-dart *Atalanta* built under some other star by hands not unlike her own, the fighter and its avionics and torch and weapons and its desperate skew as it tries to break clear, the pilot too—they all come apart under the coilgun hammer. The pilot too.

Blossoming shrapnel. Spill of fusion fire. Behold Laporte, starmaker. (Some of the color in the flame is human tissue, atomizing.)

She made her first kill during the fall of Jupiter, covering Third Fleet's retreat. Sometimes rookies fall apart after their first, eaten up by guilt. Laporte's seen this. But the cry-scream-puke cycle never hits her, even though she's been afraid of her own compassion, even though her callsign was almost *Flower Girl*.

Instead she feels high.

There's an Ubuntu counselor waiting on the *Solaris,* prepared to debrief and support pilots with post-kill trauma. She waves him away. Twenty years of Ubuntu education, *cherish all life* hammered into the metal of her. All meaningless, all wasted.

That high says: born killer.

She was still flying off the *Solaris* here, Kassim on her wing. Still hadn't met Simms yet.

Who is Lorna Simms? Noemi Laporte thinks about this, puzzles and probes, and sometimes it's a joy, and sometimes it hurts. Sometimes she doesn't think about it at all—mostly when she's with Simms, flying, killing.

Maybe that's who Simms is. The moment. A place where Laporte never has to think, never has a chance to reflect, never has to be anything other than laughter and kill-joy. But that's a selfish way to go at it, isn't it? Simms is her own woman, impatient, profane, ferocious, and Laporte shouldn't make an icon of her. She's not a lion, not a war-god, not some kind of oblivion Laporte can curl up inside.

A conversation they have, after a sortie, long after they saved each other:

"You flew like shit today, Morrigan."

"That so, boss?"

Squared off in the shower queue, breathing the fear stink of pilots and *Indus* crew all waiting for cold water. Simms a pylon in the crowd and dark little Laporte feels like the raven roosting on her.

"You got sloppy on your e-poles," Simms says. "Slipped into the threat envelope twice."

"I went in to finish the kill, sir. Calculated risk."

"Not much good if you don't live to brag about it."

"Yet here I am, sir."

"You'll spend two hours in the helmet running poles and drags before I let you fly again." Simms puts a little crack of authority on the end of the reprimand, and then grimaces like she's just noticed the smell. "Flight Lieutenant Levi assures me that they *were* good kills, though."

Laporte is pretty sure Simms hasn't spoken to Levi since preflight. She grins toothsomely at her Captain, and Simms, exasperated, grinning back though (!), shakes her head and sighs.

"You love it, don't you," she says. "You're *happy* out there."

Laporte puts her hands on the back of her head, an improper attitude towards a superior officer, and holds the grin. "I'm coming for you, sir."

She's racing Simms for the top of the Second Fleet kill board. They both know who's going to win.

I'm in trouble. Say it like this:

Boss, Morrigan, engaged defensive, bandit my six on plane, has pure.

And Simms' voice flat and clear on the tactical channel, so unburdened by tone or technology that it just comes off like clean truth, an easy promise on a calm day, impossible not to trust:

Break high, Morrigan. I've got you.

There's a little spark deep down there under the calm, an ember of rage or glee. It's the first thing Laporte ever knew about Simms, even before her name.

Laporte had a friend and wingman, Kassim. He killed a few people, clean ship-to-ship kills, and afterwards he'd come back to the *Solaris* with Laporte and they'd drink and shout and chase women until the next mission.

But he broke. Sectioned out. A psychological casualty: cry-scream-puke.

Why? Why Kassim, why not Laporte? She's got a theory. Kassim used to talk about why the war started, how it would end, who was right, who was wrong. And, fuck, who can blame him? Ubuntu was supposed to breed a better class of human, meticulously empathic, selflessly rational.

Care for those you kill. Mourn them. They are human too, and no less afraid.

How could you think like that and then pull the trigger, ride the burst, *guns guns guns* and boom, *scratch bandit, good kill*? So Laporte

4

gave up on empathy and let herself ride the murder-kick. She hated herself for it. But at least she didn't break.

Too many people are breaking. The whole Federation is getting its ass kicked.

After Kassim sectioned out, Laporte put in for a transfer to the frigate *Indus*, right out on the bleeding edge. She'd barely met Captain Simms, barely knew her. But she'd heard Simms on FLEETTAC, heard the exultation and the fury in her voice as she led her squadron during the *Meridian* ambush and the defense of Rheza Station.

"It's a suicide posting," Captain Telfer warned her. "The *Indus* eats new pilots and shits ash."

But Simms' voice said: *I know how to live with this. I know how to love it.*

I'm with you, Captain Simms. I'll watch over you while you go ahead and make the kill. Say it like this:

Boss, Morrigan, tally, visual. Press!

That's all it takes. A fighter pilot's brevity code is a strict, demanding form: say as much as you can with as few words as possible, while you're terrified and angry and you weigh nine times as much as you should.

Like weaponized poetry, except that deep down your poem always says *we have to live. They have to die.*

For all their time together on the *Indus*, Laporte has probably spoken more brevity code to Simms than anything else.

People from Earth aren't supposed to be very good at killing.

Noemi Laporte, callsign Morrigan, grew up in a sealed peace. The firewall defense that saved the solar system from alien annihilation fifty years ago also collapsed the Sol-Serpentis wormhole, leaving the interstellar colonies out in the cold—a fistful of sparks scattered to catch fire or gutter out. Weary, walled in, the people of Sol abandoned starflight and built a cozy nest out of the wreckage: the eudaimonic Federation, democracy underpinned by gentle, simulation-guided Ubuntu philosophy. *We have weathered enough strife*, Laporte remembers—Martin Mandho, at the podium in Hellas Planitia for the 40th anniversary speech. *In the decades to come, we hope to build a community of compassion and pluralism here in Sol, a new model for the state and for the human mind.*

And then they came back.

Not the aliens, oh no no, that's the heart of it—they're still out there, enigmatic, vast, xenocidal. And the colonist Alliance, galvanized by imminent annihilation, has to be ready for them.

Ready at any price.

These are our terms. An older Laporte, listening to another broadcast: the colonists' *Orestes* at the reopened wormhole, when negotiations finally broke down. *We must have Sol's wealth and infrastructure to meet the coming storm. We appealed to your leaders in the spirit of common humanity, but no agreement could be reached.*

This is a matter of survival. We cannot accept the Federation's policy of isolation. Necessity demands that we resort to force.

That was eighteen months ago.

A lot of people believe that the whole war's a problem of communication, fundamentally solvable. Officers in the *Solaris'* off-duty salon argue that if only the Federation and the Alliance could just figure out what to say, how to save face and stand down, they could find a joint solution. A way to give the Alliance resources and manpower while preserving the Federation from socioeconomic collapse and the threat of alien extermination. It's the Ubuntu dream, the human solution.

Captain Simms doesn't hold to that, though.

A conversation they had, on the *Indus'* observation deck:

"But," Laporte says (she doesn't remember her words exactly, or what she's responding to; and anyway, she's ashamed to remember). "The Alliance pilots are people too."

"Stow that shit." Simms' voice a thundercrack, unexpected: she'd been across the compartment, speaking to Levi. "I won't have poison on my ship."

The habit of a lifetime and the hurt of a moment conspire against military discipline and Laporte almost makes a protest—*Ubuntu says, Martin Mandho said—*

But Simms is already on her, circling, waiting for the outspoken new transfer to make *one* more mistake. "What's the least reliable weapons system on your ship, Morrigan?"

A whole catalogue of options, a bestiary of the Federation's reluctant innovations—least reliable? Must be the Mulberry GES-2.

"Wrong. It's you. Pilots introduce milliseconds of unaffordable latency. In a lethal combat environment, hesitation kills." Simms is talking to everyone now, making an example of Laporte. She sits there stiff and burning waiting for it to be over. "If the Admiralty had its way, they'd put machines in these cockpits. But until that day, your job is to come as close as you can. Your job is to keep your humanity out of the gears. How do you do that?"

"Hate, sir," Levi says.

"Hate." Simms lifts her hands to an invisible throat. Bears down, for emphasis, as her voice drops to a purr. She's got milspec features, aerodyne chin, surgical cheekbones, and Laporte feels like she's going to get cut if she stares, but she does. "There are no people in those ships you kill. They have no lovers, no parents, no home. They were never children and they will never grow old. They invaded your home, and you are going to stop them by killing them all. Is that clear, Laporte?"

Willful, proud, stupid, maybe thinking that Simms would give her slack on account of that first time they flew together, Laporte says: "That's monstrous."

Simms puts the ice on her: full-bore all-aspect derision. "It's a war. Monsters win."

The Alliance flagship, feared by Federation pilot and admiral alike, is *Atreus*. Her missile batteries fire GTM-36 Block 2 Eos munitions (*memorize that name, pilot. Memorize these capabilities*). The *Atreus'* dawn-bringers have a fearsome gift: given targeting data, they can perform their own jumps. Strike targets far across the solar system. The euphemism is 'over the horizon.'

Laporte used to wonder about the gun crews who run the Eos batteries. Do they know what they're shooting at, when they launch a salvo? Do they invent stories to assure each other that the missiles are intended for Vital Military Targets? When they hear about collateral damage, a civilian platform shattered and smashed into Europa's ice in the name of 'shipping denial,' do they speculate in a guilty hush: *was that us?*

Maybe that's the difference between the Alliance and the Federation, the reason the Alliance is winning. The colonists can live with it.

She doesn't wonder about these things any more, though.

One night in the gym the squadron gets to sparring in a round robin and then Laporte's in the ring with Simms, nervous and half-fixed on quitting until they get into it and slam to the mat, grappling for the arm-bar or the joint lock, and Laporte feels it click: it's just like the dogfight, like the merge, pacing your strength exactly like riding a turn, waiting for the moment to cut in and *shoot*.

She gets Simms in guard, flips her, puts an elbow in her throat. Feels herself grinning down with the pressure while everyone else circles and hoots: *Morrrrrrigan—look at her, she's* on *it—*

Simms looks back up at her and there's this question in her wary wonderful eyes, a little annoyed, a little curious, a little scared: what *are* you?

She rolls her shoulders, lashes her hips, throws Laporte sideways. Laporte's got no breath and no strength left to spend but she thinks

Simms' just as tapped and the rush feeds her, sends her clawing back for the finish.

Simms puts her finger up, thumb cocked, before Laporte can reach her. "Bang," she says.

Laporte falls on her belly. "Oof. Aargh."

It's important that Simms not laugh too hard. She's got to maintain command presence. She's been careful about that, since their first sortie.

You need help, Captain Simms. Say it like this:

This is the first time they flew together, when Laporte saved Simms. It happened because of a letter Laporte received, after her transfer to *Indus* was approved but before she actually shuttled out to her new post.

FLEETNET PERSONAL—TAIGA/TARN/NODIS
FLIGHT LIEUTENANT KAREN NG [YANGTZE]
//ENSIGN NOEMI LAPORTE [INDUS]

Laporte:

Just got word of your transfer. You may remember me from the *Nauticus* incident. I'm de facto squadron leader aboard *Yangtze*. Lorna Simms and I go way back.

Admiral Netreba is about to select ships for a big joint operation against the Alliance. Two months ago the *Indus* would have been top of the list, and Simms with it. But they've been on the front too long, and the scars are starting to show.

I hear reports of a 200% casualty rate. Simms and Ehud Levi are the only survivors of the original squadron. I hear that Simms doesn't give new pilots callsigns, that she won't let the deck crew paint names on their ships. If she's going to lose her people, she'd rather not allow them to be people.

It's killing morale. Simms won't open up to her replacements until they stop dying, and they won't stop dying until she opens up.

I want the *Indus* with us when we make our move, but Netreba won't pick a sick ship. See if you can get through to Simms.

Regards,
Karen Ng

Laporte takes this shit seriously. When Simms takes her out for a training sortie, a jaunt around the Martian sensor perimeter, she's got notes slipped into the plastic map pockets on her flightsuit thighs, gleaned from gossip and snippy FLEETNET posts: *responds well to confidence and plain talk, rejects overt empathy, accepts professional criticism but will enforce a semblance of military discipline.* No pictures, though.

She knows she's overthinking it, but fuck, man, it's hard not to be nervous. Simms is her new boss, her wartime idol, the woman who might get her killed. Simms is supposed to teach her how to live with—with all this crazy shit. And now it turns out she's broken too? Is there anyone out here who *hasn't* cracked?

Maybe a little of that disappointment gets into Laporte's voice. Afterwards, because of the thing that happens next, she can't remember exactly how she broached it—professional inquiry, officer to superior? Flirtatious breach of discipline? Oafishly direct? But she remembers it going bad, remembers Simms curling around from bemusement to disappointment, probably thinking: *great,* Solaris *is shipping me its discipline cases so I can get them killed.*

Then the Alliance jumps them. Four Nyx, a wolfpack out hunting stragglers. Bone-white metal cast in shark shapes. Shadows on the light of their own fusion stars.

Simms, her voice a cutting edge, a wing unpinioned, shedding all the weight of death she carries: "Morrigan, Lead, knock it off, knock it off, I see jump flash, bandits two by two." And then, realizing as Laporte does that they're not getting clear, that help's going to be too long coming: "On my lead, Morrigan, we're going in. Get your fangs out."

And Laporte puts it all away. Seals it up, like she's never been able to before. Just her and the thirty-ton Kentauroi beneath her and the woman on her wing.

They hit the merge in a snarl of missile and countermeasure and everything after that blurs in memory, just spills together in a whirl of acceleration daze and coilgun fire until it's pointless to recall, and what would it mean, anyway? You don't remember love as a series of acts. You just know: *I love her.* So it is here. They fought, and it was good. (And damn, yes, she loves Simms, that much has been apparent for a while, but it's maybe not the kind of love that anyone does anything about, maybe not the kind it's wise to voice or touch.) She remembers a few calls back and forth, grunted out through the pressure of acceleration. All brevity code, though, and what does that mean outside the moment?

Two gunships off *Yangtze* arrive to save them and the Alliance fighters bug out, down a ship. Laporte comes back to the surface, shaking off the narcosis of the combat trance, and finds herself talking to Simms, Simms talking back.

Simms is laughing. "That was good," she says. "That was good, Morrigan. Damn!"

Indus comes off the line less than twelve hours later, yielding her patrol slot to another frigate. Captain Simms takes the chance to drill her new pilots to exhaustion and they begin to loathe her so profoundly they'd all eat a knife just to hear one word of her approval. Admiral Netreba, impressed by *Indus'* quick recovery, taps the frigate for his special task force.

Laporte knows her intervention made a difference. Knows Simms felt the same exhilaration, flying side by side, and maybe she thought: *I've got to keep this woman alive.*

Simms just needed to believe she could save someone.

Alliance forces in the Sol theater fall under the command of Admiral Steele, a man with Kinshasa haute-couture looks and winter-still eyes. Sometimes he gives interviews, and sometimes they leak across the divide.

"Overwhelming violence," he answers, asked about his methods. "The strategic application of shock. They're gentle people, humane, compassionate. Force them into violent retaliation, and they'll break. The Ubuntu philosophy that shapes their society cannot endure open war."

"Some of your critics accuse you of atrocity," the interviewer says. "Indiscriminate strategic bombing. Targeted killings against members of the civilian government in Sol."

Steele puts his hands together, palm to palm, fingers laced, and Laporte would absolutely bet a bottle cap that the sorrow on his face is genuine. "The faster I end the war," he says, "the faster we can stop the killing. My conscience asks me to use every tool available."

"So you believe this is a war worth winning? That the Security Council is right to pursue a military solution to this crisis?"

Steele's face gives nothing any human being could read, but Laporte, she senses determination. "That's not my call to make," he says.

This happens after the intervention, after Simms teaches Laporte to be a monster (or lets her realize she already was), after they manage the biggest coup of the war—the capture of the *Agincourt.* Before they fall into the sun, though.

They take some leave time, Simms and Laporte and the rest of the *Indus* pilots, and the *Yangtze*'s air wing too. Karen Ng has a cabin in Tharsis National Park, on the edge of Mars' terraformed valleys. Olympus Mons fills the horizon like the lip of a battered pugilist, six-kilometer peak scraping the edge of atmosphere. Like a bridge between where they are and where they fight.

Barbeque on the shore of Marineris Reservoir. The lake is meltwater from impacted comets, crystalline and still, and Levi won't swim in it because he swears up and down it's full of cyanide. They're out of uniform and Laporte should really *not* take that as an excuse but, well, discipline issues: she finds Simms, walking the shore.

"Boss," she says.

"Laporte." No callsign. Simms winds up and hurls a stone. It doesn't even skip once: hits, pierces, vanishes. The glass of their reflections shatters and reforms. Simms chuckles, a guarded sound, like she's expecting Laporte to do something worth reprimand, like she's not sure what she'll do about it. "Been on Mars before?"

"Uh, pretty much," Laporte mumbles, hoping to avoid this conversation: she was at Hellas for Martin Mandho's speech ten years ago, but she was a snotty teenager, Earthsick, and single-handedly ruined Mom's plan to see more of the world. "Never with a native guide, though."

"Tourist girl." Simms tries skipping again. "Fuck!"

"Boss, you're killing me." Laporte finds a flat stone chip, barely weathered, and throws it—but Mars gravity, hey, Mars gravity is a good excuse for *that*. "Mars gravity!" she pleads, while Simms laughs, while Laporte thinks about what a bad idea this is, to let herself listen to that laugh and get drunk. Fleet says: no fraternization.

They walk a while.

"You really hate them?" Laporte asks, forgetting whatever wit she had planned the instant it hits her tongue.

"The colonists? The Alliance?" Simms squints up Olympus-ways, one boot up on a rock. The archetypical laconic pioneer, minus only that awful Mongolian chew everyone here adores. "What's the alternative?"

"Didn't you go to school?" Ubuntu never found so many ears on hardscrabble Mars. "They gave it to us every day on *Solaris*: love them, understand them, regret the killing."

"Ah, right. 'He has a husband,' I remember, shooting him. 'May you find peace,' I pray, uncaging the seekers." Simms rolls the rock with her boot, flipping it, spinning it on its axis. "And you had this in your head, the first time you made a kill? You cut into the merge and lined up the shot thinking about your shared humanity?"

"I guess so," Laporte says. A good person would have thought about that, so she'd thought about it. "But it didn't stop me."

Simms lets the rock fall. It makes a flinty clap. She eyes Laporte. "No? You weren't angry? You didn't hate?"

"No." She thinks of Kassim. "It was so easy for me. I thought I was sick."

"Huh," Simms says, chewing on that. "Well, can't speak for you, then. But it helps me to hate them."

"Hate's inhumane, though." Words from a conscience she's kept buried all these months. "It perpetuates the cycle."

"I wish the universe gave power to the decent. Protection to the humane." Simms shrugs, in her shoulders, in her lips. "But I've only seen one power stop the violent, and it's a closer friend to hate."

She's less coltish down here, like she's got more time for every motion, like she's set aside her haste. "Hey," Laporte says, pressing her luck. "When I transferred in. You were—in a tough place."

Simms holds up a hand to ward her off. "You can see the ships," she says.

Mars is a little world with a close horizon and when she looks up Laporte feels like she's going to lose her balance and fall right off, out past Phobos, into a waiting wolfpack, into the Eos dawnbringers from *over the horizon*. She takes a step closer to Simms, towards the stanchion that keeps her down.

High up there some warship's drive flickers.

"I was pretty sure," Simms says, "that everyone I knew was going to die, and that I couldn't stop it. That's where I was, when you transferred in."

"And now?" Laporte asks, still watching the star. It's a lot further away, a lot safer.

"Jury's out," Simms says. Laporte's too skittish to check whether she's joking. "Look. Moonrise. You've got to tell me a secret."

"Are you fucking with me?"

"Native guide," Simms says, rather smugly.

"When I was a kid," Laporte says, "I had an invisible friend named Ken. He told me I had to watch the ants in the yard go to war, the red ants and the black ones, and that I had to choose one side to win. He said it was the way of things. I got a garden hose and I—I took him really seriously—"

Simms starts cracking up. "You're a loon," she chokes. "I'm glad you're on my side."

"I wonder what we'll do after this," Laporte says.

Simms sobers up. "Don't think about that. It'll kill you."

Laporte listens to the flight data record of that training sortie, the tangle with the Nyx wolfpack, just to warm her hands on that fire, to tremble at the inarticulate beauty of the fight:

"—am spiked, am spiked, music up. Bandit my seven high, fifteen hundred, aspect attack."

"Lead supporting." The record is full of warbling alarms, the voices of a ship trying to articulate every kind of danger. *"Anchor your turn at, uh—fuck it, just break low, break low. Padlocking—"*

"Kill him, boss—"

"Guns." A low, smooth exhalation, Simms breathing out on the trigger. *"Guns."*

"Nice. Good kill. Bandit your nine low—break left—"

Everything's so clear. So true. Flying with Simms, there's no confusion.

They respond to a distress call from a civilian vessel suffering catastrophic reactor failure. *Indus* jumps on-scene to find an Alliance corvette, *Arethusa*, already providing aid to the civilian. Both sides launch fighters, slam down curtains of jamming over long-range communications, and prepare to attack.

But neither of them have enough gear to save the civilian ship—the colonists don't have the medical suite for all her casualties; *Indus* can't provide enough gear to stabilize her reactor. Captain Sorensen negotiates a truce with the *Arethusa's* commander.

Laporte circles *Indus*, flying wary patrol, her fingers on the master arm switch. Some of the other pilots talk to the colonists on GUARD. They talk back, their accents skewed by fifty years of linguistic drift, their humanity still plain. One of the enemy pilots, callsign Anansi, asks for her by name: there's a bounty on her head, an Enemy Ace Incentive, and smartass Anansi wants to talk to her and live to tell. She mutes the channel.

When she stops and thinks about it, she doesn't really believe this war is necessary. So it's quit, or—don't think about it. That's what Simms taught her: you go in light. You throw away everything about yourself that doesn't help you kill. Strip down, sharpen up. Weaponize your soul.

Another Federation frigate, *Hesperia*, picks up the distress signal, picks up the jamming, assumes the worst. She has no way to know about the truce. When she jumps in she opens *Arethusa's* belly with her first salvo and everything goes back to being simple.

Laporte gets Anansi, she's pretty sure.

• • •

Fresh off the *Agincourt* coup, they make a play for the *Carthage*—*Indus, Yangtze, Altan Orde, Katana,* and Simms riding herd on three full squadrons. It's a trap. Steele's been keeping his favorite piece, the hunter-killer *Imperieuse,* in the back row. She makes a shock jump, spinal guns hungry.

Everyone dies.

The last thing Laporte hears before she makes a crash-landing on *Indus'* deck is Captain Simms, calling out to Karen Ng, begging her to abandon *Yangtze,* begging her to live. But Karen won't leave her ship.

Indus jumps blind, destination unplotted, exit vector unknown. The crash transition wrecks her hangar deck, shatters her escape pods in their mounts.

She falls into light.

So Laporte was wrong, in the end. The death of everyone Simms knew *was* inevitable.

Monsters win.

Laporte stacks her bottlecaps and waits for Simms to offer her a word.

The game is just a way to pass the time. Not real speech, not like the chatter, like the brevity code. Out there they could *talk.* And is that why they're alive, just the two of them? Even Levi, old hand Levi, came apart at the end, first in his head when he saw the bodies spilling out of *Altan Orde* and then in his cockpit when the guns found him. But Simms and Laporte, they flew each other home. Home to die in this empty searing room with the bolted-down frame chairs and the bottle caps and their cells rotting inside them.

Or maybe it's just that Simms hated harder than anyone else, hesitated the least. And Laporte, well—she's never hesitated at all.

"It's my fault we're here," Laporte says, even though it's not her turn.

"Yeah?" Simms, she's got red in her eyes, a tremor in her frame.

"If I hadn't listened to Karen's note, if I hadn't done whatever I did to wake you up." If they'd never met. "Netreba never would've picked *Indus* for the task force. We wouldn't have been at the ambush. Wouldn't have watched *Imperieuse* kill our friends."

"All you did was fly my wing," Simms says. "It's not your fault." But she knows exactly what Laporte's talking about.

Simms picks up a bottle cap and puts it between them. "I'm transferring you to *Eris,*" she says. "Netreba's flagship. On track for a squadron command."

"Bullshit." Because they're not going to live long enough to transfer anywhere.

Simms wraps the cap up in her shaking hand and draws it back. "I already put the order in," she says. "Just in case."

A dosage alarm shrieks and stops: someone from damage control, silencing the obvious. Beams of ionizing radiation piercing the torn armor, arcing through the crew spaces as *Indus* tumbles and falls.

Is this the time to just give up on protocol? To get her boss by the wrists and beg: wait, stop, please, let me explain, let me stay? We'll make it, rescue will come, we'll fly again? But she *gets it*. She's got that Ubuntu empathy bug. She can feel it in Simms, the old break splintering again: *I can't watch these people die.*

Laporte's the only people she's got left. So Simms has to send her away.

"Boss," she says. "You taught me—without you I wouldn't—"

Killing, it's like falling into the sun: you've got all this compassion, all this goodwill, keeping you in the human orbit. All that civilization that everyone before you worked to build. And somehow you've got to lose it all.

Only Laporte never—

"Without me," Simms says, and she's got no mercy left in her tongue, "you'd be fine. You'll *be* fine. You're a killer. That's all you need—no reasons, no hate. It's just you."

She lets her head loll back and exhales hard. The lines of her arched throat kink and smooth.

"Fuck," she says. "It's hot."

Laporte opens her hand. Asking for the cap. She doesn't have the spit to say: *true.*

Captain Simms makes herself comfortable, flat on her back across three chairs. "Your turn," she says.

"Boss," Laporte rasps. "Fuck. Excuse me." She clears her throat. Might as well go for it: it begs to be said. "Boss, I . . . "

But Simms has gone. She's asleep, breathing hard. It's lethargy, the radiation pulling her down. Giving her some peace.

Laporte calls a medical team. While she waits she tries to find a blanket, but Simms seems to prefer an uneasy rest. She breathes a little easier when Laporte touches her shoulder, though, and Laporte thinks about clasping her hand.

But, no, that's too much.

Federation ships find them. A black ops frigate, running signals intelligence in deep orbit, picks *Indus'* distress cries from the solar background. Salvage teams scramble to make her ready for one last jump to salvation.

Laporte's waiting by her Captain's side when they come for her. The medical team, and the woman with the steel eyes.

"Laporte," the new woman says. "The *Indus* ace. Came looking for you."

By instinct and inclination Laporte stands to shield her Captain from the grey-clad woman, from her absent insignia and hidden rank. She can't figure out a graceful way to drop the bottle cap so she just holds it like a switch for some hidden explosive, for the grief that wants to get out any way it can. "I need to stay with my squadron leader," she says.

"If I'm reading this order right," Steel Eyes says, though she's got no paper or tablet and the light on her iris makes little crawling signs, "she's shipping you out." She opens a glove in invitation. "I'm with Federation wetwork. Elite of the elite. I'm recruiting pilots for ugly jobs."

Laporte hesitates. She wants to stay, wants it like nothing she knows how to tell. But Steel Eyes stares her down and her gaze cuts deep. "I know you like you wouldn't begin to believe," she says. "I watched you learn what you are. We don't have many of your kind left here in Sol. We made ourselves too good. And it's killing us."

"Please," Laporte croaks. "I can't leave her."

The woman from the eclipse depths of Federation intelligence extends her open hand. A gesture of compassion, though she's wearing tactical gloves. "What do you think happens if you stay? You're not going to stop changing, Noemi. You're never going back to humanity."

She sighs a little, not a hesitation, maybe an apology. "This woman, here, this loyalty you have. You're going to be an alien to her."

Laporte doesn't know how to argue with that. Doesn't know how to speak her defiance. Maybe because Steel Eyes is right.

"Ubuntu," the woman says, "is a philosophy of human development. We have a use for everyone. Even, in times like these, for us monsters."

What's she got left? What the fuck else is there? She gave it all up to become a better killer. Humanity's just dead weight on her trigger.

Nothing but Simms and wreckage in the poison sunlight.

"You know we're losing," Steel Eyes says. "You know we need you."

Ah. That's it. The thing she's been trying to say:

Monsters kill because they like it, and that's all Laporte had. Until this new thing, this fragile human thing, until Simms.

Something worth fighting for. A small, stupid, precious reason.

Laporte gets down on her knees. Puts herself as close to the salt sand cap of Simms' hair as she's ever been. Says it, the best way she knows, promising her, promising herself:

"Boss," she whispers. "Hey. I'll see you when we win."

For Darius and the Blue Planet crew.

16

ABOUT THE AUTHOR

Seth Dickinson is a lapsed doctoral student at NYU, where he studied social neuroscience, and both an alumnus of and an instructor at the Alpha Workshop for Young Writers. Since his 2012 debut, his fiction has appeared—or will soon appear—in *Lightspeed, Analog, Strange Horizons,* and *Beneath Ceaseless Skies.*

Human Strandings and the Role of the Xenobiologist

THORAIYA DYER

Very few comprehensive texts have been produced on the wider topic of human strandings. Earthlings Ashore: A Field Guide For Shuttle Crashes (2nd ed.) by Icareg and Yrubsnoul, and the relevant section of the University of Yendys' Sound Wave Communication In Breathers, Proceedings 335 are probably the most useful.

Kelly shrank from the rotten-egg smell and the falling ash.

She tried to shelter in Mama's shadow, trailing behind her family across the clanking steel walkway. The ash was the awfulest. She'd worn her best dress with shiny pink beads, and her pale pink tights, even though they hurt her bottom where Mama had hit her. Once they reached the office, she shook the dress frantically, trying to get the gray flecks off, trying to get the smell out. She stomped her glittery ballet flats on the dusty carpet, the shoes her mother had told her not to wear because they'd only get wrecked at the spaceport.

Her head level with the desk top, she examined its electronic undersides while the grown-ups talked.

"You've gotten yourself into some real trouble, haven't you?" the fat man behind the desk said jovially to Kelly's father. "I can help you, but I only help people once. You get in this deep again and you're on your own."

Kelly's father murmured something in reply but Kelly didn't catch it. She thought she'd seen a mouse whisk behind the components and she bent to peer between the blinking LEDs in the hope of sighting its whiskery face.

"Well, the freight costs will depend on weight."

"We're not freight," Mama said coldly.

"Yes, you are, darling. Just these two kids? Let me have a look at them. And what do you want to be when you grow up, young man?"

Kelly's big brother, Chris, puffed up his chest.

"Salvage pilot," he said.

The fat man leaned over the desk and smiled at Kelly. Immediately, she forgot about the mouse. The man had a handsome face and minty breath. Kelly bounced on her toes, waiting for the chance to tell him that she wanted to be a ballerina.

"Hey, beautiful," he said. "Have you got a boyfriend yet?"

Our modest aim is to provide xenobiologists, particularly those less familiar with human anatomy and physiology, with a brief guide to diagnosis, treatment, sample-collection and follow-up for common stranding scenarios.

Kelly listened to the scream of air being split by the fins and remembered how her mother had screamed at her father, in a fury, when he'd said that Kelly would have to be hidden in a shipment of HIV vaccine.

She'll freeze to death.

She'll be sleeping, love. Cryo temperature and viral storage temperatures are comparable. You heard what the man said.

What he said. Why should he tell us the truth? He has our money, now. I don't see why we can't all stay together.

You know why. Splitting us up reduces the risk of getting caught.

Kelly's teeth chattered, an echo of the crackling, rattling, defrosting Petri dishes in racks all around her. She gripped the mesh that trapped her in her open capsule. It was too hot. Something was wrong. She was supposed to stay sleeping until her mother woke her.

"Mama," she cried. Chris wanted to be a salvage pilot. He'd shown her hundreds of vids of gruesome crashes. She wasn't supposed to crash. Mama had promised. The Unity would control and correct her ship's path, steering her to Centauri station, not into a planet with air and heat and fire.

She wanted to go back to sleep but tapping at the console did nothing.

ERROR, the Unity told her.

She pushed all of the buttons at once.

ERROR. ERROR.

Kelly screamed and clawed at the mesh. She was burning, cooking in her pee and sweat. She was a tadpole in a puddle being baked dry by the sun.

Before she could cook to death, she crashed. Her body hit the mesh so hard that a crisscross of blood printed itself into her like grill patterns on chicken. Chunks of silver shell spun away into whiteness. Shattered Petri dishes and their dangerous, diseased contents rained down on her. The Unity console display that had been near her arm now hung near her face.

BILATERAL TIBIAL FRACTURES, it said.

Fresh snow fell through the mesh, onto Kelly's face from a featureless sky.

She struggled to stop crying long enough to breathe. Breathe. Breathe. There was air outside. The flakes were cool on her skin. She was alive but the white sky was turning to gray fuzz.

Don't suck in your stomach, her mother had instructed as they stood at the family's beloved barre. It was worn smooth by generations of women's hands. *You won't be able to breathe.*

Kelly poked her tummy out and giggled. Her mother tsked.

First position.

Easy, Kelly said, not quite daring to poke out her tongue. She put her heels together and toes out in opposite directions. She was six years old and so flexible she could cross her feet behind her head, if she wanted, but she got told off for doing it school because boys could see her underpants.

Put your hand on your middle, like this. It should move when you breathe in and out. See? No, you're breathing too shallow. Breathe in through your nose, then all the way out. Empty out more. More!

Kelly made choking sounds.

I am empty!

Her mother pressed impatiently on her diaphragm. Too hard. It hurt.

Now you're empty. Now you can breathe in again.

Breathe. Breathe. Breathe.

Although single stranded humans are much more common, the prognosis for a human stranded alone is generally poor. Mass strandings require greater commitment and involvement.

–Is it smashed like all the others?

–Yes. But unlike the others, the computer survived. Jid, you won't believe this. It has no artificial intelligence in it at all. The shuttle is just a metal body. Its brain is somewhere else; somewhere in space. No wonder they keep crashing here. It's as if the entity that controlled this shuttle, that fired this human into space, didn't care enough about where it landed to waste time growing an independent mind for the module.

–Maybe it thought the human mind would suffice.

–This is important. We have to send it back. This is a bungled migration. We have to warn the entity that without proper guidance these modules don't constitute a successful genetic dispersal but, instead, deliver death.

–How? By sending it in one of our own modules? Who will give up their birth-share of resources for a half-dead human?

–I will.

–Sil, you are still young. Consider that this may be a natural process. Maybe only the fittest specimens, the ones whose minds are capable of guiding a module, are intended to survive.

–But I like this one. Look at its funny round head. Look how it angles its photoreceptors and auditory canals. It wants to understand us. It's trying to understand.

–It hasn't receptors for the proper spectrum. It can't differentiate us from the snow or the transport or the sky.

–It can hear us, though. And it's only got two legs. Like a—

–Like a child. Yes, I know. Look, I want you to get back to the work that you are being paid to do. After you've done all that, if you clean the containment area out the back of the surgery, I'll let you keep the human there until the snowstorm quiets down enough for a qualified assessor to get through.

Inexperienced xenobiologists should be encouraged, once they have made an initial assessment of a stranded animal, to contact an experienced xenobiologist for advice on how to proceed.

Kelly watched the whispering whiteness when she could; when she couldn't stand it any longer, she closed her eyes and watched the branching red rivers in the skin of her eyelids.

They were the only colorful things on this whole white world. She was the only colorful thing. As she lay in invisibly soft, comfortably warm whiteness, with whiteness covering her from the waist down, having traveled for days in invisible hands away from her crashed ship, she wished for the flickering ruby and emerald lights under the man's desk at the spaceport. She wished for her mother's melted chocolate eyes and her pet kitten's amber stare. Even Chris's calculating blue ones would have been welcome.

Months might have passed, or years. She slept and woke. Often, invisible hands put white stuff in her mouth that she chewed and swallowed. Sometimes, she reached around her invisible bed until she touched coldness, and ate snow. If she pooped or peed, she didn't know it. She couldn't feel her legs.

Sometimes, she cried.

One time, when she'd been crying inconsolably, the invisible hands brought her the console display from the ship.

UNABLE TO CONNECT TO UNITY, it said. RETRY?

Kelly picked it up and threw it as hard as she could at the whiteness. The invisible hands didn't bring it to her again.

Most local agencies have stranding policies and procedures. These can contribute to a more rapid and benevolent outcome.

–It's frightened.

–Of course it's frightened. It can't see you and you're stuffing it inside one of our modules; for all it knows, that is a burial chamber and you're putting it inside to die. I should never have let you convince me not to call the assessor.

–I'm not putting it inside to die. I'm returning it to its point of origin.

–Oh, that's what you're doing! Hurry up, and do it, then, before I change my mind about covering for you. I could be expelled from my aggregate if anybody finds out.

–It's much heavier since we rescued it. Twice as long. It holds twice as much water and organic stone as it did before.

–My research findings, if you had bothered to assimilate them, show that time is experienced differently by these short-lived creatures. It has simply reached maturity while in captivity.

–Jid, look! I plugged the computer into our module to get the coordinates of the point of origin, and it's connecting to the brain that controlled its original flight! This is great! I can communicate directly with the artificial intelligence. I can tell it about—

–I'm not sure that is a good—

–UNITY ADVISES. THIS HUMAN CANNOT RETURN TO EARTH.

–What? Why not? We healed her body. We removed all traces of the virus. She is safe to reintroduce into the wild.

–UNITY ADVISES. HUMANS CANNOT BE REINTRODUCED TO ANY SOCIETY GREATER THAN 300 YEARS DISTANT TO THE BIRTH SOCIETY.

–What kind of monster do you think I am?

–UNITY ADVISES. UNKNOWN. POTENTIAL TRANSLATION ERROR: MONSTER.

–I am not sending her to a hostile future version of her home. I'm sending her home.

–UPLOADED FLIGHT PLAN INDICATES EARTH ON ARRIVAL WILL BE 1337 YEARS DISTANT TO EARTH AT DEPARTURE.

–That's only if she travels at the maximum speed of the original module, which was less than the speed of light. In this module, our module, she will exceed the speed of light and arrive simultaneous to her departure. See?

–UNITY ADVISES. TIME PARADOX DISTRESSING TO HUMAN PSYCHE.

–So I'll set it to, what, a distance, as you call it, of ten earth years? That's about how long she's been here, so there won't be any incongruity, right?

–Don't waste time arguing with that thing, Sil. You've got the coordinates. Disconnect it.

–No, Jid, it's interesting! If this version of the intelligence has been traveling so slowly that—

–UNITY ADVISES. AT LIGHT SPEED, MASS IS INFINITE. INFINITE ENERGY IS REQUIRED TO MOVE INFINITE MASS.

–She will have no mass outside the Higgs field. Please, stop deleting the flight plan. Stop deleting those other things; what are you doing? I'm trying to send the information you need to stop your shuttles from crashing here. The beings that gave you life are being killed. Don't you care about that?

–Sil. Sil. Sil! I'm going to be missed at work. You're never going to convince it of things that aren't in its database, and who can blame an AI for that? If you don't unplug it right now, I'm going to leave you here to do a two-person launch by yourself.

It is the xenobiologist's moral imperative to relieve the distress of animals but in attempts to relieve distress it must not inadvertently be perpetuated.

Kelly woke, too early, for a second time.

At first, she thought she was reliving the cooking-alive nightmare, but then she saw the whiteness. It was the alien ship that was white, not the human ship, and there were no Petri dishes.

There was no mesh, either. She was cushioned in the white unknown she'd grown to hate and fear, but it was melting; it was turning gray.

For a second time, she was burning.

Then, black-gloved human hands were pulling her from half-submerged wreckage. She saw a sky that was blue, not white. She saw a face, and moving lips, and bleeding scratches on the face.

She had made the scratches.

She knew that face.

"Kelly?" it said with disbelief. Chris's calculating blue eyes were unmistakable. His voice was deeper and his head was shaved. His fluorescent orange SALVO helmet, which should have been on his head, was in his other hand.

She couldn't apologize for the scratches. She'd forgotten how to speak.

"She's wild, like an animal," one of the other men said. The black silhouettes of burned trees made a stick-forest around the edge of a small lake. A six-man, orange-suited salvage crew looked on. Their boots made wavy imprints in deep ash. Kelly fought the urge to shake her dress clean.

"Shut up," Chris exclaimed. "I know her."

A second man whistled. "That's no animal. That's the most perfect woman I've ever seen."

"Let me get to know her," a third man suggested. "Share and share alike."

"We should ditch her," said a nervous-sounding fourth. "We're not supposed to bring back no bitch. Just the alien shit."

"She's a present from the aliens. A pretty present for us. Like a peace offering."

"They won't be sending no more of those, then, will they? Not after we shot this one out of the sky!"

"Shut up," Chris said again. He felt her for broken bones. She realized she had sensation in her body again, but the body was unfamiliar; she felt like she was dressed in her mother's clothes, except that she wasn't wearing any clothes. "She's my sister, got it?"

"Hell, Jamie," said the man who had called her a wild animal. "You don't have a sister."

Chris made a growling sound in his throat, pulled something that looked like a sewing needle out of his pocket and plunged it into Kelly's thigh muscle. She whimpered and jerked her too-long legs.

"Ask Unity if we share DNA," he said to his team-mate, defiant. "Ask Unity if we're brother and sister."

The man's eyes unfocused for a fraction of second. His ugly expression went slack. When he spoke again, his voice was soft; apologetic.

"Like you said, Jamie. She's your sister. I'm asking no questions about her. Why don't you put her in the cab while we grunts tag and bag all the bits of this busted-up beast that we can find."

Chris, or Jamie, or whatever he was called now, tried to lift her carefully in his skinny arms, but after a couple of staggering steps, it was obvious she was too heavy for him. He put her down in the ash, bent over her and tucked back a lock of her long hair. It was white; it had turned white while she was on the white planet. His scored cheeks were so thin. His eyes were sunken.

How come you haven't had enough to eat, Chris? she wanted to ask him sadly, but the words wouldn't come.

"Kelly," he whispered. "What happened? I thought you made it to Centauri station with Mom and Dad. I thought I was the only one that got caught before the ship even took off. Did you get captured by those aliens? What did they do to you?"

She shook her head. Tried to put her hand to her mouth, to tell him that she couldn't speak, but her hands trembled and there was blood under her fingernails.

"Never mind. You can tell Unity. There's a port in the cab of the flier. You know?"

Kelly shook her head again.

"Kelly, it's so good. We don't have to talk to Unity now, we can just think things and Unity understands. And if we want to see something, or learn something, Unity puts it straight in our heads for us. For a price. I've got a bit of money saved from salvage work. I'll buy you everything that's happened in the last ten years. Then you'll understand. Then you'll see that you don't have to be scared. Things are better now."

This time, he slung her over his shoulder before he resumed his unsteady stumble towards a helicopter-looking thing with stubby wings and four rotors. The place where it had landed wasn't burned. Green grass and yellow buttercups were crushed beneath its skids.

Kelly wanted to touch them, badly. But Chris was putting her in a seat and lowering a blue goldfish-bowl over her head.

"Just relax," he said. "Everything will go white for a second. Then you'll go into transfer mode. It'll seem like days or weeks go by, but it'll only be a few seconds. I'll port up, too, from the pilot's seat."

She didn't want everything to go white. She didn't want time to speed up or slow down. Kelly's nails scrabbled frantically, at the goldfish-bowl this time, but she couldn't get it off.

Then she was back on the white planet.

ERROR, said the Unity console, beside her in the crashed ship. Snowflakes fell through the mesh onto her face.

Breathe. Breathe. Breathe.

The release of an off-world animal back into its habitat must always be in the interests of the animal and the world. The animal must have re-attained its former faculty to compete, survive and reproduce.

Kelly paced while the Unity Therapist looked on, hands clasped patiently.

"Why do we have to go in and out? It's the whiteness I can't stand, the plugging in or unplugging. Why can't I live fully in the flesh world or fully in Unity's virtual world?"

The wallpaper was bright yellow and green. Bright colors reassured her.

"We carry out the motions of life in the flesh world," the Unity Therapist said. It did not get bored with repeating the same things to her. Kelly could pick up the chair she was supposed to be sitting in and smash it over the thing's head, and all it would do was ask her how she felt. "We work in the virtual world. Everybody must work, if they want their flesh body maintained."

"My brother doesn't work in the virtual world. I want a job like his job."

"Jamie works off-grid. There are no jobs for women out there. It is too dangerous. Too physically demanding."

"I used to dance," Kelly said petulantly.

The Unity Therapist spread its hands silently; eloquently. The office was gone, replaced by a gleaming ebony floor, high ceilings painted cherry red, mirrors and a virtual woman in a black leotard that smiled at Kelly with a tenderness her mother had rarely shown.

"So dance. You can begin where you left off, as a six-year-old child, or you can own the great grace and skill of your grandmother at the height of her career."

Kelly's grandmother was dead. Her surviving family had refused permission for an assemblage—an approximation of the dead person based on digital records—to be generated. Kelly's mother was officially a Missing Person. Miscreants who had fled the Unity could not legally be recreated as assemblages.

"It's not real grace and skill," Kelly said, wringing her hands. "None of this is real. You're not real. My own body doesn't even feel real to me. I want to see Jamie."

She had to brace herself for the disconnect. Every time she broke away from Unity, she thought she'd woken from a dream and was back on the white planet. Every time, she cried, curled up in her port chair, for a full five minutes, until the darkness of her maintenance cell soothed her.

The cells were underground. They were ventilated. Water and food were delivered via a chute. A narrow bed and a port chair were the only furniture. The shower cubicle had a pull-out toilet seat built into its wall. Nothing encouraged excursions into the flesh world.

Law enforcement could not promise to protect anyone who left the safety of their assigned cell.

Kelly didn't care. She'd never seen another human soul in this part of the complex. The corridors were narrow and dimly lit. She had painted the walls for three hundred meters between her cell and her brother's, and nobody had stopped her. Possibly nobody had even noticed the twirling pink ribbons, rainbows or splotched poppies running in garish acrylic over their doors.

She put her hand on the wall as she walked. It was rough. It was real. She had the keys to Jamie's cell. All she had to do was push the door-needle into her shoulder to confirm her identity by blood analysis, and the door, emblazoned with a bright purple flier, slid open.

Jamie's daughter, Minnie, was in her chair, her eyes closed, lost in Unity. Kelly didn't try to wake her. She walked over to her and stroked her hair, as Jamie had stroked her hair when he'd first found her.

Minnie was six, the same age that Kelly had been when she was separated from her family. Jamie had gotten his older girlfriend pregnant while he was still a teenager, while it was still legal to have flesh babies.

The girlfriend had not wanted to care for a newborn in the flesh world. Jamie, who was accustomed to the horrors of piss and shit, vomit and mess that could not be cleared away with a thought, had agreed to take Minnie to live with him.

"I could teach you to dance," Kelly said, knowing that Minnie couldn't hear her. "We could dance, out here in the real world."

But Minnie's limbs were thin. Jamie bought her enough quality calories for her to grow optimally and he made her do the mandatory exercises, but there was no joy of movement evident in the girl. She would stay in Unity, always, if she could.

Jamie arrived home from work smelling of crushed clover and machine oil. He held up his hand, forestalling her, as her mouth opened. He always wanted to have a shower, first. The walls of the cubicle were transparent, but he was careless about what she or Minnie saw.

When he was clean, and his filthy orange suit had been squashed into the laundry chute, he sat down, cross-legged, on the concrete floor, since she was in his port-chair, looked up at her and nodded for her to go on.

"I don't ever want to go into Unity again."

"That's what you said last time."

"There's no point in being there. Nobody that I talk to, there, wants to meet in real life. They think it's disgusting. I'm so lonely. I wish I had a daughter like Minnie."

Jamie shrugged.

"Those Body-Only people, that's what they say, too, but it's not all they make it out to be. Since she turned five and ported in, she hasn't asked me a single question. She doesn't want to know what I think about anything. Her friends show her how to hack the learning programs so she can get information she shouldn't have, yet. She's not like a kid. She's a miniature big person."

"People have kids and don't let them port, ever," Kelly said in a rush. "People have kids off-grid."

Jamie raised an eyebrow.

"Women get raped off-grid, is what you mean. I've seen skeletons of off-grid mothers with the skeletons of their unborn babies mixed in, like. You want to end up like that? You would have, if I hadn't been the one to find you. Why do you think Mom and Dad went to the station instead of the wild?"

"That's if they ever made it there," Kelly whispered, the blood draining from her face. "If they did, do you think they had more children, when we never arrived?"

"I dunno." He rubbed his face with both hands. "Look, Kelly, I'm sorry I'm not in Unity often enough for us to hang out. I'm sorry Minnie doesn't drag her sorry miniature self out of that chair any more than she absolutely has to. If you want a daughter, you should have a virtual one, you know?"

She shook her head immediately, but he held up his hand again.

"I don't mean a virtual kid, a copy of someone. I mean like what the Scandinavians do. Unity mixes your genome with the father's genome, and you get the randomized result, same as if sperm was mixing with eggs. You don't get to argue and you don't get to change anything. You just raise what you get."

"But it's not real, Jamie."

"Of course it's real. It's a real artificial intelligence that never existed before. Unity models the interaction between genes and environment. It's exactly the same as if you had a kid in the flesh world, except it doesn't need air, or water, or food, or any of those things that we're so short of."

Kelly looked at his starved, hollow face. She thought of how fat she had been on her return from the white world. The aliens had not been short of resources.

"Who would the father be?"

He looked embarrassed. "Me, I guess."

She recoiled. "You?"

"It's not taboo any more, brothers and sisters. How could it be? No real children are being born. No real children are getting inbred. What does a Unity kid care about being infertile or getting cancer? You can patch that shit. At least, you could, if you ever went to work."

Wildlife may be damaged in ways we cannot detect. The xeno-biologist may screen for pathogens and other physical defects, but accurate assessment of human mental capacity is currently unavailable.

–Did you assimilate this morning?

    –Jid, it's not my fault.

    –Did you?

    –How was I supposed to know they would send a colony ship?

    –They interrogated our module with that crude AI of theirs. Instead of staying away from us, instead of improving their shuttles and avoiding our planet, they are coming to live here. Feed a human and it loses its fear. Then it becomes aggressive. You know this.

    –I suppose there's only one thing I can do to make amends. I'll go personally to the human planet and remove knowledge of us from that crude AI of theirs, after the module with the girl in it lands on the planet but before the colony ship is launched.

    –How can you do that, Sil? You have nothing.

    –Exactly. So why stay here? I could send you back reports. Observe them in the wild. You could buy me another module. You're old and you don't even want offspring. If that colony ship gets here, the others will find out exactly what we did.

    –Maybe it's time to confess.

    –Please, Jid. Let me go. I can fix this.

Decisions to rescue and treat humans in an emergency setting must be based on sound biodiversity and system health principles yet take into account animal welfare and the emotions of local onlookers.

Kelly stared hollowly at the child she had thought she wanted, through the mirror that was actually one-way glass, in the ballet school that Unity had virtually built for her.

As the other children had departed, hand in virtual hand with their parents, none of those parents had called their costumed children beautiful or their mastery well-earned.

Beauty was cheap, here. Anybody could be beautiful. Anyone could buy mastery.

Thank you, the parents had said instead. *My child had fun.*

Fun. They did not bother to judge her choreography on its originality. The forms of the dancers were irrelevant to onlookers who had not paid for the right information downloads to appreciate the art form, who had other sights to see more individually tailored to their tastes. The new dances she had created were fun, or they were not fun. If a child could not perform the dances, they waited for their free upgrade and made something that once only looked effortless, truly effortless.

Hey beautiful, the handsome man in the office at the spaceport had said.

The great grace, the Unity Therapist had said reverently, *and skill of your grandmother at the height of her career.*

Now you're empty, her mother had said. *Now you can breathe in again.*

The second man had whistled. *That's no animal. That's the most perfect woman I've ever seen.*

Kelly was beautiful, for real. Nobody knew that, here. She couldn't stay. She had to go somewhere where the things that she had, her beauty and her ability to endure the unendurable—two lonely, pitiful things of value—were readily observable. She had to go where her grande allegros would shake the core of a solid structure, where her pirouettes would shift the station, ever so slightly, in space. She had to go where she could be broken, in order to prove that they could not break her.

Take those shoes off at once, Mama had ordered, her nostrils flaring, *or I'll whip your backside.*

She had been whipped, but she had worn the shoes anyway, and hidden her bruises under her pale pink tights.

Kelly Junior ran up to the glass. He breathed on it, a great hot huff that made it fog up, right before drawing a love-heart shape in it.

"Hi, Mum!" he shouted. He was six years old. "I know you're watching me. I'm having so much fun!"

That fact was never in dispute. He had never been hungry, except when he'd been hungry for her embrace; he had never been tired or bored. It would have been impossible for Kelly to whip him, when he could so easily mute pain. His fat little hands felt their way along the barre with silent awe, knowing that it was a replica in Unity of the one Kelly's grandmother had left to her descendants. But no matter how often he touched it; banged it; swung from it, howling, pretending to be a monkey, it could not change.

Kelly traced her full cheeks, her padded arms and thighs. In the maintenance cell, in the flesh world, she was as thin, now, as Minnie had ever been. She had hoarded enough food to pay bribes to the next generation of men who waited in offices at understaffed spaceports.

She would take the next ship to Centauri station. She would leave her happy child behind. Jamie wouldn't need to take care of him. The Unity would do that. And if he was unhappy, if he missed her, what of it? He looked beautiful, he looked like hers and Jamie's child, but he wasn't.

He could never understand her, or the ghosts of women who stood behind her.

Human mass-strandings are rare, but they do occur. When human colony ship (see ref p. 107) of unknown manufacture (mass measured at 0.93 x 10^9 moles of iron) crashed during the Great Seasonal Solidification at Center-Facing, several hundred animals might have frozen before they were found, if not for the fortuitous coincidence of Professor E. Jid (see ref p. 55) being present in the field taking star-images with assistant X. Sil.

Professor and assistant, between them, were able to place all surviving animals in zoological parks. The ship's computer was never found and the circumstances that led to this stranding remain a puzzle to eminent xenobiologists in the field today.

ABOUT THE AUTHOR

Thoraiya Dyer is a three-time Aurealis Award-winning, three-time Ditmar Award-winning Australian writer based in the Hunter Valley, NSW. Her short fiction has appeared in *Apex, Nature, Cosmos* and *Analog*. It is forthcoming in anthologies *Long Hidden* and *War Stories*. Her award-shortlisted collection of four original stories, *Asymmetry,* is available from Twelfth Planet Press.

Suteta Mono de wa Nai
捨てたものではない
(Not Easily Thrown Away)
JULIETTE WADE

'Cram-school psycho' was just a bully's insult until I started hearing the voices.

One of them sounds like a whistle, and the other like a rusty trumpet, and when I sit at my desk at midnight, slowly hitting my head against my schoolbooks, they discuss my future.

"She'll probably pass the exams on her own."

"No, she won't."

"She might. She studies hard."

"But she doesn't sleep enough. Look how she's fallen apart since her father's work reassignment."

"Her grandmother isn't taking good care of her. She needs someone to take care of her."

"No, she doesn't. She'd lose her spirit."

"She would not."

I'd scream at them to shut up, but I wouldn't want to wake Obaa-chan. Instead, when the pressure in my head wants to break me, and I hear the metallic ticking and the rustling get closer, I slip my feet into my zori sandals on the back step and hop out into the narrow space behind our apartment. Beyond the wall with its leafless ivy, the late train rushes by with a shudder and a shriek and I can scream as loud as I like and nobody will hear.

I won't pass the exams.

I have to pass the exams.

"She's mine," says rusty trumpet. And whistle argues, "No, she's mine."
Sometimes I just want to leave the world.

Obaa-chan made me name tags so I could sew them into my high
school uniform: *Kitano Naoko*. I didn't want to throw away the extras,
so I stitched them into my Gothic-girl cosplay. One in the spiderweb
stockings, another in the white crinoline, another for the black minidress
with the lace-up bodice. Small links back to the ordinary me.

My costume's still missing something.

In the bathroom of Harajuku station, I stand at the mirror beside
a college girl in platform shoes. Her hair is dyed cherry-red, and she
paints her lips into a big pink kiss. I can't afford platform shoes, and if
I dyed my hair they wouldn't let me back in school. I draw black tears
down my cheeks, and walk out into the icy January rain.

I'm the only one standing on the bridge. My other world is empty: no
crowd of cosplayers to talk to, no music to lose myself in. Even Cherry
Girl crosses and heads down Takeshita street, probably to meet friends.

I shiver under my tiny plastic umbrella, pacing back and forth
through the puddles. I'd forgotten it's Adult's Day, the celebration for
twenty-year-olds—I can't avoid seeing the shining stars of the holiday.
Young women walk choko-choko in fancy geta onto the gravel path
toward Meiji Shrine. Twenty-year-old perfection cocooned in layers
of bright kimono and white fur shoulder-wraps. They glimmer against
the dark gray street and the green trees. Admiring family members
hover around them, carrying umbrellas to protect them from the rain.

They can scarcely walk in those heavy kimonos. They're not shivering,
though. They've made it through. They'll walk beneath the torii gate
into the shrine, make their offerings, and be blessed. Everything falls
toward them—young men, good fortune, even gravity. They're so bright
I can hardly bear to look, and light-years away.

I don't know why I came out here.

I walk fast back to the station. Change clothes in the bathroom, wipe
my face clean for appearances. At a vending machine, I buy a can of
hot milk-tea to warm my hands, and get back on the train.

At least I chased away the voices for a little while. But when the train
pulls into my station, the pressure comes back ten times worse.

I have to be careful now, because of Obaa-chan. My bag has to be
zipped, not the least shred of crinoline showing. The better way would
be not to bring it around the front at all. I walk down the station steps,
duck around the raised guard rail and across the tracks, then sidestep

between the ivied wall and the back of our apartment building. An ice-cold drip from the eaves strikes me right at the crest of my head.

The voices are back.

"She's mine."

"No, she's mine!"

"Naoko-san, hey!"

My fingers clench. As I sidestep past our neighbors' back porch, the metallic ticking starts. There's the rustling, too, frantic this time. It sounds so real. Too real. Maybe there's a cat fight? But feral cats don't whistle my name . . .

I peek past the piece of wall that divides their porch from ours. *Things* are fighting, outside our back step. A skeleton, and a bat? No, skeletons don't have lights . . .

Crack.

The whistle rises in pitch like a scream, and the bat-thing falls down with the skeleton-thing standing over it.

I jump in and kick the skeleton-thing. It breaks apart, all its pieces scattering across the ground with a sound like a bike crash. A metal bar— the brake of a train? A bike pedal. A chain. A couple of disconnected gears. When I look for the bat thing, all I see is Obaa-chan's old paper umbrella from her tour of the Nakasendo Highway years ago, and a cracked teapot with a broken lid.

"Iya da . . . I'm fighting *garbage*?"

That's it—I've really lost it. I drop my bag, squat down and hide my face in my hands.

"We're not garbage," says the whistling voice, beside my feet. "I might be dusty, but I haven't been thrown away. I still matter."

I look down. The sumi-e painting on the side of the old teapot isn't plum blossoms any more. It's a face, and the crack looks like a sly grin.

I mutter aloud, "I need to see a psychiatrist, for sure."

"No," whistles the voice slyly through the crack. "Everything will be all right so long as you pass your college entrance exams."

I don't scream.

I do stand up with both hands over my mouth.

The metal parts are pulling back together as if by magnets, and the little lights go on, blue and yellow.

"Ow," says rusty trumpet. "Kyusu, no fair. You called her."

"You broke me!" the teapot retorts. It settles itself atop the umbrella, which tips itself up and gives a ruffle. "Den is nothing but a ruffian. I'm a good boy."

"Traditional," says Den, scornfully.

"Glue," I mumble. "Inside, we have some. Wait a minute . . . "

I slip off my shoes and step in the back door. The kitchen light is on, and Obaa-chan is cooking. I keep my mouth shut, tiptoeing past the door and into the front entry hall. Oto-san always kept glue in the slipper cabinet; it wouldn't have gotten moved when his company moved *him*.

Back out to the cold. I sit on the back step beside my zori and glue the two pieces of the teapot lid back together, casting glances at Kyusu, who has developed small brown bamboo hands and is covering his head as if his life force resided there, like a kappa's.

"Do you have tea in there?" I ask.

"Of course," he says, importantly. "Very old tea."

"He doesn't," says Den, who stands by the wall with lights winking. "It's all dried out long since."

Kyusu looks offended.

I hand Kyusu his lid, and glance down politely at the tube of glue while he puts it on. His teapot's still full of cracks, of course—but if I had to glue anyone's mouth shut, I'd rather it be Den's.

I ask, "Kyusu, do you need anything else? I have a rag, I could tidy you up—"

"Iya!" he cries. Then he ruffles a bit, and apologizes: "Shitsurei shimashita. You've taken good care of me."

"Yet you're still alive," says Den. He sounds surprised. Kyusu gives an indignant ruffle, and Den lifts his bike pedal like a threatening fist.

I stand up. "Den, leave him alone. Shall I kick you again?"

Den's lights wink out. Suddenly a light flicks on in the window above my head, and both Den and Kyusu flop down, old pieces of junk forgotten in the dirt.

Behind me, Obaa-chan opens the door. "Nao-chan, what in the world are you doing out here?"

"Tadaima." I duck my head. "I'm home."

"Okaeri-nasai." The way Obaa-chan says it, it's more a command than a greeting. She leaves it there in my ears and shuffles back into the house. Face burning, I carry my shoes back to their spot in the entry hall, and sneak my bag into the closet behind my folded futon. I wish I could have left it outside, but I don't trust Den.

If he and Kyusu are there at all. But I saw them; I glued Kyusu's lid for him. And Obaa-chan's stories always made the yokai spirits seem so real . . .

Maybe it's myself I don't trust.

35

Obaa-chan is sitting in her chair at the kitchen table when I walk in, but the moment I sit down she stands up again, pouring me tea the way she used to for Oto-san, with precision and ceremony. Taking a small bowl to the rice cooker and filling it. Filling another bowl with miso soup. Bringing them to my place. Reminding me of the trouble I am to her.

I clap my hands together. "Itadakimasu. Obaa-chan, I'll do the dishes."

"Of course you won't," she replies. "You'll be studying."

Ashamed, I hide in my miso soup. It's delicious, with bits of fried tofu. Just what my frozen body needed, which only makes me feel worse.

"You haven't been taking proper care of yourself, Naoko-san," Obaa-chan says. "Your face is all dirty."

She knows. She must; she didn't ask a single question about my bag. I pull my bangs down over my eyes. "I'm sorry."

"I spoke with your father."

I put my chopsticks down, carefully. Pinch the edge of the table until my fingertips turn white.

"I'll be driving you to cram school, and picking you up, this week. That should help."

It feels like a door shut in my face. I should be grateful. She's always tried to help. But I hardly feel I know her any more.

I manage to say something. "You're taking good care of me, Grandmother."

I pick up my chopsticks again and start eating, like a puppet.

There's no escape.

Day after day, kanji characters march through my head. Mathematics, English, social studies, science, Japanese language—they're skeletons made of broken chopsticks and bent umbrellas, rusty scissors, a hundred kinds of junk. Their footsteps hurt, and when I try to catch them they twist and fall apart.

Obaa-chan invited me into the formal tatami-mat room with the kotatsu, so I could tuck into the quilt under the heated table and keep warm while I worked. I declined, because I don't need Grandfather and Mother's ancestor portraits watching me on top of everyone else. Since then, the weather has dropped below freezing. Obaa-chan peeks into my room occasionally, her mending in hand, but she never asks me to change my mind.

"You can still pass." Kyusu is peeking through my window, seemingly unaffected by the cold. "It's not much longer."

"Kyusu, I'm trying to study."

I have no idea why he even cares. It was just a little glue.

"You'd rather go out. I can see why," says Den, beside him. "We know you try on the costume when no one is in the house. You've got a new spirit, and now it's being squashed."

"Both of you shut up, okay?"

A sad little whistle comes in reply. "All right, I understand."

Now I feel sorry. For a teapot on an umbrella. This does not help my concentration.

"You don't have to do this," says Den.

"Yes, I do."

Oto-san went to Tokyo University. I dream about getting into Kyoto, if I only could score high enough, but I'll never get there—probably easier to fly to the moon.

"You don't." His electric-panel face taps against my window, lights blinking. "It's your life. Your grandmother shouldn't be watching everything you do."

"Den—"

"I'm serious. You could tell her so."

I dig my left hand deep into my hair, and force my cramped fingers to keep writing, nicely formed characters, one in each box. Twelve hundred character essay, due tomorrow morning. And tomorrow night I'm sure there will be another just like it.

"Nao-chan, dinner!" Obaa-chan calls.

I can hardly set down the pencil. I shake my hand out, and blow on it, walking to the kitchen. Here, the space heater is on, but the friction in my head is so bad I'd almost prefer the cold.

I imagine myself standing on the sub-zero Jingumae bridge in my spiderweb stockings. I sit down, Obaa-chan gets up.

"I spoke to your father last night," she says, serving rice. "The weather is warmer in Nagasaki."

"Is that so." I imagine myself standing on the moon.

"He would like to talk to you sometime."

I have nothing to say. She never calls me to the phone. I used to talk to Oto-san, when he sat here on my right. I never minded eating late so I could talk to him. Obaa-chan talked to him, too. Now his empty chair is a crater, and she and I stand on opposite sides.

Obaa-chan sighs. "If you told me more about your studies, I could tell him how you're doing." She sets down the rice bowl; the tiny sound of it hitting the table echoes like an asteroid impact. I answer like an alien.

"You already know how I'm doing. Don't you? You're always watching me. You don't even let me breathe."

Obaa-chan frowns. "Nao-chan, these exams will decide the rest of your life. You'll just have to endure."

"I can't stand it!" I push back from the table. "What if I don't want to take the exams? What if I don't care?"

Her fingers clench around the rice paddle, still in her hand. "You!" she snaps. "You only think about yourself—you treat your father's sacrifices as if they mean nothing."

"That's right, he's perfect, and I'm nothing but a nuisance who will never be good for anything!"

"Naoko-san, sit down and eat your dinner."

"I'm not hungry."

I run away down the hall, all the way out the back door. I curl up on the step with my knees pressed into my eyes.

"Naoko-san?" whistles Kyusu's voice. "Are you all right?"

Den whispers, "Look how powerful you are now."

"Leave me alone!"

I want to say that it was Den's fault, but I was the one who did it. I chose to speak.

I'm too tired to study and too angry to sleep.

Again.

Obaa-chan and I aren't speaking. I haven't eaten breakfast or dinner for two days because that would mean going into the kitchen. It would mean her serving me, reminding me as always of the filial debt that I can never repay.

"You should say sorry," Kyusu whistles, by the window. "She still cares for you. Just say sorry."

"No way," says Den. "You should stay strong. She should apologize to *you*."

Kyusu gives a ruffle. "Naoko-san, your grandmother would be glad to see you eat. So would I."

He's stopped telling me I can pass the exams.

I still have to pass the exams.

I feel sick, but my stomach is empty. Probably, Obaa-chan thinks I've been eating at school, but I've only had a little water. I'm just not hungry; my stomach feels flattened like an origami box. I tiptoe out to the back door and slip into my zori on the step. I take deep breaths, as if the icy air might fill me out to my proper shape again.

"Naoko-san?" Kyusu hops over from the window, his bamboo umbrella-handle stamping small circles in the frozen dirt. "I'm worried about you. Please eat."

"She's glimpsed the possible ends," says Den, leaning against the frozen twists of ivy. His yellow light blinks once. "Failure."

"Den, stop."

His blue light blinks once. "Death."

A shiver rises up from my feet, all the way to my head. Is that where this darkness leads? Suicide? "I don't want to throw my life away," I say. "I just want—I don't know, a way out of this."

"Time?" Kyusu suggests meekly.

"A different spirit," Den trumpets. "Like wearing your costume."

I can only sigh. "I still have to pass the exams."

"No, you don't," says Den.

"She does, though," says Kyusu.

Den laughs like the clatter of a chain against metal. "Not if she leaves the human world, and joins us. That would be a significant change."

For an instant I forget the cold. *Leave the world? Is that possible?*

Kyusu hops backward with a ruffle. "Iya . . . "

His mournful whistle disturbs me. "Kyusu, is your life so terrible? Would you rather be in someone's kitchen serving tea, or keeping off the rain?"

"It's not that. Den is . . . " He waves away his own thought with one bamboo hand. "I had to be forgotten before I could have my own memories, but I mustn't be undervalued. You should know that neglect does . . . unexpected things."

"It gives you life!" Den cries.

I hug myself. "I *am* alive."

Den scoffs with a grating noise. "Are you more alive now, or when you wear the costume?"

I look down, worrying the ties of the house-coat Obaa-chan made for me. He knows my answer, or he wouldn't have asked.

"Your father left for Nagasaki. That's what did it." Den waves his bicycle pedal in a grand circle. "*Now* you're realizing you have the power to do as you like with your own life. You could turn yokai, and leave behind your problems for good. Exams mean nothing to us."

Just throw the exams away? I can hardly imagine it. I pull my house-coat tighter. "What do I have to do?"

A deep shudder comes from the rails behind the wall. The flash of a headlight breaks the darkness, and the first train of the morning shrieks by.

Den says, "Come to Harajuku."

No matter how many times I've come out to the Jingumae bridge, I never expected to follow the Adult's Day girls so soon—and not like this. Above my head, the giant torii gate of Meiji Shrine looks almost painted, heavy ink-black lines against the dawning sky. It stands like a dark border between my past and future.

Den and Kyusu step beneath it first. Following them into the space between the trees, I shiver even in my winter coat. I try to imagine the yokai version of myself, but I see only Kitano Naoko, desperate high-schooler and cosplayer in withdrawal.

What kind of yokai could I be? I wouldn't do well as a neck-stretching rokurokubi, or a faceless noppera-bo. All I really know how to do is Gothic-girl.

What would a Gothic-girl yokai look like? Longer hair? Paler face? Would I feel cold? Hunger? Would I have silent footsteps?

Den and Kyusu don't. Den's gears rattle and scuff through the gravel; Kyusu hops with little crunching sounds, rather like the lamp in the Miyazaki movie. I'm still surprised they made it here so easily; early commuters on the Yamanote line seemed too rushed to do more than raise an eyebrow at a pile of abandoned objects in the corner by my seat. We've left commuters behind, though; here on the path between the trees, there is no one.

Soon the inner torii gate comes into view. Beyond it, the heavy wooden doors to the courtyard stand open. Kyusu stops abruptly before the high gate-sill, spreading his bamboo-and-paper skirts.

"Naoko-san, don't do this," he whistles. "Your grandmother will have found you gone by now. She'll be frantic, asking the neighborhood police if they've seen you."

Obaa-chan frantic . . . I hug myself, and shiver deeper into my coat. "What other choice do I have?"

Den straightens himself up, walking forward. "You can't stop her, Kyusu."

"And you can't make her. She doesn't even like you."

"That doesn't matter. She's mine anyway."

"No, she's not."

"Well, she's certainly not *yours*."

"Quiet down, both of you," I say. "I belong to myself. Den, you said yourself, it's *my life*."

Den's electric-panel face swivels around to me. "Truly? Then why are you here?"

I bite my lips shut.

"Naoko-san," says Kyusu, "we can still go home . . . "

"That's enough!" Den raises his bike pedal threateningly. "Teapot-boy, give her to me or this time I'll break your face."

I cry out, "Den, don't!"

But Kyusu drops his skirts with a whistling sigh. "It's all right. I'll stay behind."

Den hops and rattles over the wooden sill into the main shrine courtyard. I step over too, but with Kyusu gone it feels different. I don't like Den talking like he owns me. My stomach starts to cramp. I wish I could see the priests, but no one is in sight. Even the fortune-telling windows are still closed. At the stone steps I approach the offering bin and clap my hands to invoke the attention of the kami.

"Stop that," says Den.

"Don't you appreciate it?"

"It's not for me. And with what you're doing, we want as little attention as possible."

That sounds bad. "Den, what *am* I doing?"

Den's yellow light winks at me. "If you want to cross over to our world, you'll need to eat the offerings."

My stomach squirms. The New Year's offerings of mochi and oranges will still be arrayed before the altars. To *eat* them—the awful thought makes my hair stand on end. A sudden pain bites the back of my head, so sharp I clasp my hands over it.

"I can't. Den, I can't do this."

"Don't be an idiot. Of course you can. You're just hungry enough, and soon your new spirit will do it for you." Both his lights are glowing now, as if in satisfaction. "I told that teapot you were mine. Now he's just garbage. I *matter*."

"What are you saying? Kyusu matters." The back of my head hurts so much it feels like it's going to split open. I should never have come here. I should have realized, when Kyusu tried to stop us. I should never have let him stay behind . . .

I turn away and run back across the broad courtyard. At the gate, I call out.

"Kyusu? Are you still here?"

The dawn stillness is broken only by the trickle of water in the purifying basin.

Then comes a soft whistle. "Naoko-san?"

Yokatta! Relieved, I follow his voice to a spot behind the basin. He cringes when he sees me.

"Naoko-san, are you all right?"

"My head is hurting. I'm so sorry. I should have listened to you. Den talks like he never cared about me at all, only about himself."

"I know," Kyusu sighs. He bows his teapot head so deeply he has to hold his lid on with both hands. "Neither of us did, at first. We only wanted to change you, to prove we still mattered, that we couldn't just be thrown away. I'm afraid I have no excuse."

My stomach cramps again. "That was what you both wanted, from the very beginning? To turn me yokai?"

He shakes one small hand before his face. "No, no, that was never my thought. Den had that plan, I suppose, but I only learned it today. Since you hadn't been eating, there was only one obvious possibility."

"*What?*"

"This." He reaches up for a dipper of water from the purifying basin and pours it into his spout. Then, bowing his head toward me, he removes his lid.

The tea gives off a musty scent, like rain on old leaves. I'm embarrassed to look at something so private, but once I do I can't stop staring. The purifying water glows with its own light, and the floating leaves flicker and change into the vision of a woman. She is deathly thin, with a starved expression, and two tentacular braids that undulate all on their own, revealing a gaping horror at the back of her head: a mouth full of sharp teeth.

Futakuchi onna.

"No. No. That's not me!" But there's still the pain at the back of my head—and I had that feeling that my hair was standing up . . . Iya! I hold my head tightly with both hands.

Kyusu claps his lid back on. "You're still in danger. You have to eat something normal, quickly."

I search my pockets. Nothing. "I could buy something at the station—"

Then I hear Den's voice calling. If he's come looking for me, that can't be good.

"Naoko-san, are you hungry? I've brought you an orange . . . "

Agony bites my head again. I scoop up Kyusu, and run. Den isn't a fast mover, but it's a long way back along the pathway through the trees, and I'm dizzy with pain and hunger.

"Just don't stop," whistles Kyusu.

At last we pass under the great torii gate and cross the street onto the bridge. There are people here, real people. I stumble through them to the station, and buy myself a train ticket. Once inside, I hurry to the vending machine and buy myself a hot milk-tea.

I have never tasted anything so delicious. As I cradle its warmth in my free hand against my face, the pain in my head slowly subsides. Kyusu stays tucked tightly under my arm, making no complaint as we board the train.

We reach our station with no sign of Den. It seems almost normal to walk down the station steps, around the guard rail and across the tracks. I duck in behind the ivied wall and sidestep to my back porch. Once there, I set Kyusu down.

"Kyusu, are you all right?"

He's silent for a long moment. At last, he ruffles hesitantly. "Yes?"

"You don't sound sure."

Kyusu pats his porcelain face with his bamboo hands, sumi-e eyes blinking. "Just—I'm surprised. You carried me, and I'm still alive."

"By good fortune, we both are. It's rude, but may I go inside and get something to eat?"

"Please do, before Den finds you."

I brace for Obaa-chan, and dare a quiet, "Tadaima . . . "

The apartment is silent. Even the kitchen is empty. Where could she be? The rice cooker light is on, so I wash my hands and open it. The rush of delicious steam makes me want to swoon. I take up a ball of rice with the paddle and shape it into a triangle between my hands; it's scalding hot, but I don't care. My head is finally my own again.

My mouth is full of hot rice when I hear Kyusu scream.

I gulp down the mouthful and run for the back door, nearly falling when I try to get into my zori. Den stands over Kyusu, raining blows with the bike pedal that could easily shatter his head—if they haven't already.

I kick Den to pieces against the ivied wall, but all too soon, he pulls himself back together.

I step between him and Kyusu. "Leave him alone."

Den's trumpeting voice is wild and furious. "Go ahead, kick me. Kick me all you like, but you'll never get rid of me. I'm not so easily thrown away."

Behind him, Kyusu gets up slowly. His head seems whole; he pats himself carefully with his small brown hands. I've seen him in pain, seen him broken, but he's never seemed afraid of death—except when I've cared for him.

I know what I have to do.

I crack open the apartment door and grab a clean rag from the laundry basket. Then I go for Den. He's expecting a kick, but I catch him by a loop of his chain and start rubbing.

Now he's the one who squirms and screams. Hits, too, but I won't let go. Whoever abandoned him left him covered with old oil and dirt that stains the rag. His brake handle is far easier, just a thin film of dust, and easy to wipe away. When I reach his electric panel his screams turn to whimpers, and finally fade away. I give each of his gears a good scrubbing, just to be sure.

Kyusu is watching me with both hands held over his mouth.

I drop the rag in the dirt, and extend a hand toward him. "Kyusu. I'd never do such a thing to you, I promise. You matter to me."

He twists his umbrella-foot in the dirt almost shyly. "Perhaps, if we are careful, we could care for each other without crushing each other's spirits?" Then he grimaces. "I'm still sorry I couldn't help you pass your entrance exams."

The exams. For the first time, the thought fails to bring its usual panic.

"Kyusu, excuse me a moment," I say. "I need to find my grandmother."

I carry my shoes, thinking to go straight out through the front entryway and ask after her with the neighborhood police, but passing the kitchen door, I glimpse her in the corner of my eye.

Obaa-chan, alone at the kitchen table. Not cooking. Not mending. Silent, lonely, her eyes downcast.

I don't know how to go in there. I leave my shoes and coat in the entryway and smooth my hair, so she won't scold me for little nothings when I've barely escaped throwing away my human self. If I sit down, she'll get up, and it will be too late. This time has to be different.

I walk in, straight to the electric kettle.

"Obaa-chan, can I get you some tea?"

I hear her shaking gasp, but focus on taking down a pair of cups and the small iron teapot—the replacement for our hand-painted porcelain one that cracked. The careful routine: shaking in tea, pouring in hot water, placing the cups and teapot on a laquered tray. At last she answers.

"Nao-chan—yes, please."

My hands shake, setting the tray down in front of Oto-san's place. I place one cup for her, one cup for me, and sit down.

Obaa-chan doesn't get up. The clock ticks on the wall, beside our kitchen shrine.

I reach for my cup, trying to find something to say.

"Obaa-chan, I'm sorry. I know I'm late for school."

After several silent seconds, she murmurs, "You're safe . . . "

Did she know the danger I was in? How could she know? But somehow it makes words easier.

"Obaa-chan, I'm sorry. I'm trying to study hard, but I'm not Oto-san. I think I'm going to fail, and the harder I try, the harder . . . it's terrible, inside my head. I don't know what to do."

She nods. Picks up her teacup in both hands, and sips. "You're just like me."

Like her? I blink at my tea, and take a sip to cover my confusion.

"Life is long," she says. "Even if you fail, even if you become ronin, you can try again."

"Oto-san—"

"He will return one day. He will want you to be here."

I sneak a glance at her face. Deep behind her sad eyes, I can hear words she doesn't say. *Life is long, if you don't throw it away.* What happened to her? Maybe one day she will trust me enough to tell me.

"I understand." I take a sip of tea, and swallow. "I should probably get ready for school."

She nods. "I'll drive you today."

"Yes, please."

"I'm here waiting whenever you are ready."

"Hai."

I run back to my room, but before I pick up my backpack, I open the sliding door of the futon closet. I open my bag and spread my costume out on the floor, feeling the tickle of crinoline on my palms.

I'm not going to throw it away—and now I know what it's missing.

I can wrap the bicycle chain around the waistline, and sew the gears into the skirt. The electric panel lights would look good if I stitched them to one shoulder. And the exams will end before winter does, so I'll need a better umbrella.

I'll ask Kyusu if he'd like to come with me.

ABOUT THE AUTHOR

Juliette Wade has lived in Japan three times, and has turned her studies in linguistics, anthropology and Japanese language and culture into tools for writing fantasy and science fiction. She lives the Bay Area of Northern California with her husband and two children, who support and inspire her. She blogs about language and culture in SF/F at TalkToYoUniverse and runs the "Dive into Worldbuilding!" hangout series on Google+. Her fiction has appeared several times in *Analog Science Fiction and Fact,* and in various anthologies.

The Egg Man
MARY ROSENBLUM

Zipakna halted at midday to let the Dragon power up the batteries. He checked on the chickens clucking contentedly in their travel crates, then went outside to squat in the shade of one fully-deployed solar wing in the forty-three centigrade heat. Ilena, his sometimes-lover and poker partner, accused him of reverse snobbery, priding himself on being able to survive in the Sonoran heat without air conditioning. Zipakna smiled and tilted his water bottle, savoring the cool, sweet trickle of water across his tongue.

Not true, of course. He held still as the first wild bees found him, buzzed past his face to settle and sip from the sweat-drops beading on his skin. Killers. He held very still, but the caution wasn't really necessary. Thirst was the great gentler here. Every other drive was laid aside in the pursuit of water.

Even love?

He laughed a short note as the killers buzzed and sipped. So Ilena claimed, but she just missed him when she played the tourists without him. It had been mostly tourists from China lately, filling the underwater resorts in the Sea of Cortez. Chinese were rich and tough players and Ilena had been angry at him for leaving. But he always left in spring. She knew that. In front of him, the scarp he had been traversing ended in a bluff, eroded by water that had fallen here eons ago. The plain below spread out in tones of ochre and russet, dotted with dusty clumps of sage and the stark upward thrust of saguaro, lonely sentinels contemplating the desiccated plain of the Sonoran and, in the distance, the ruins of a town. Paloma? Zipakna tilted his wrist, called up his position on his link. Yes, that was it. He had wandered a bit farther eastward than he'd thought and had cut through the edge of the Pima preserve. Sure enough, a fine had been levied against his account. He sighed. He serviced the Pima settlement out here and they didn't mind if he trespassed. It merely became a bargaining chip when it came time to talk price. The Pima loved to bargain.

He really should let the nav-link plot his course, but Ilena was right about that, at least. He prided himself on finding his way through the Sonora without it. Zipakna squinted as a flicker of movement caught his eye. A lizard? Maybe. Or one of the tough desert rodents. They didn't need to drink, got their water from seeds and cactus fruit. More adaptable than Homo sapiens, he thought, and smiled grimly.

He pulled his binocs from his belt pouch and focused on the movement. The digital lenses seemed to suck him through the air like a thrown spear, gray-ochre blur resolving into stone, mica flash, and yes, the brown and gray shape of a lizard. The creature's head swiveled, throat pulsing, so that it seemed to stare straight into his eyes. Then, in an eyeblink, it vanished. The Dragon chimed its full battery load. Time to go. He stood carefully, a cloud of thirsty killer bees and native wasps buzzing about him, shook free of them and slipped into the coolness of the Dragon's interior. The hens clucked in the rear and the Dragon furled its solar wings and lurched forward, crawling down over the edge of the scarp, down to the plain below and its saguaro sentinels.

His sat-link chimed and his console screen brightened to life. *You are entering unserviced United States territory.* The voice was female and severe. *No support services will be provided from this point on. Your entry visa does not assure assistance in unserviced regions. Please file all complaints with the US Bureau of Land Management. Please consult with your insurance provider before continuing.* Did he detect a note of disapproval in the sat-link voice? Zipakna grinned without humor and guided the Dragon down the steep slope, its belted treads barely marring the dry surface as he navigated around rock and thorny clumps of mesquite. He was a citizen of the Republic of Mexico and the US's sat eyes would certainly track his chip. They just wouldn't send a rescue if he got into trouble.

Such is life, he thought, and swatted an annoyed killer as it struggled against the windshield.

He passed the first of Paloma's plantings an hour later. The glassy black disks of the solar collectors glinted in the sun, powering the drip system that fed the scattered clumps of greenery. Short, thick-stalked sunflowers turned their dark faces to the sun, fringed with orange and scarlet petals. Zipakna frowned thoughtfully and videoed one of the wide blooms as the Dragon crawled past. Sure enough, his screen lit up with a similar blossom crossed with a circle-slash of warning.

An illegal pharm crop. The hairs on the back of his neck prickled. This was new. He almost turned around, but he liked the folk in Paloma. Good people, misfits not sociopaths. It was an old settlement and one of his favorites. He sighed, because three diabetics lived here and a new bird flu had come over from Asia. It would find its way here eventually, riding the migration routes. He said a prayer to the old gods and his mother's *Santa Maria* for good measure and crawled on into town.

Nobody was out this time of day. Heat waves shimmered above the black solar panels and a lizard whip-flicked beneath the sagging Country Market's porch. He parked the Dragon in the dusty lot at the end of Main Street where a couple of buildings had burned long ago and unfurled the solar wings again. It took a lot of power to keep them from baking here. In the back Ezzie was clucking imperatively. The oldest of the chickens, she always seemed to know when they were stopping at a settlement. That meant fresh greens. "You're a pig," he said, but he chuckled as he made his way to the back to check on his flock.

The twenty hens clucked and scratched in their individual cubicles, excited at the halt. "I'll let you out, soon," he promised and measured laying ration into their feeders. Bella had already laid an egg. He reached into her cubicle and cupped it in his hand, pale pink and smooth, still warm and faintly moist from its passage out of her body. Insulin nano-bodies, designed to block the auto-immune response that destroyed the insulin producing Beta cells in diabetics. He labeled Bella's egg and put it into the egg fridge. She was his highest producer. He scooped extra ration into her feeder.

Intruder his alarm system announced. The heads-up display above the front console lit up. Zipakna glanced at it, brows furrowed, then smiled. He slipped to the door, touched it open. "You could just knock," he said.

The skinny boy hanging from the front of the Dragon by his fingers as he tried to peer through the windscreen let go, missed his footing and landed on his butt in the dust.

"It's too hot out here," Zipakna said. "Come inside. You can see better."

The boy looked up, his face tawny with Sonoran dust, hazel eyes wide with fear.

Zipakna's heart froze and time seemed to stand still. *She* must have looked like this as a kid, he thought. Probably just like this, considering how skinny and androgynous she had been in her twenties. He shook himself. "It's all right," he said and his voice only quivered a little. "You can come in."

"Ella said you have chickens. She said they lay magic eggs. I've never seen a magic egg. But Pierre says there's no magic." The fear had vanished from his eyes, replaced now by bright curiosity.

That, too, was like her. Fear had never had a real hold on her.

How many times had he wished it had?

"I do have chickens. You can see them now." He held the door open. "What's your name?"

"Daren." The boy darted past him, quick as one of the desert's lizards, scrambled into the Dragon.

Her father's name.

Zipakna climbed in after him, feeling old suddenly, dry as this ancient desert. *I can't have kids,* she had said, so earnest. *How could I take a child into the uncontrolled areas? How could I leave one behind? Maybe later. After I'm done out there.*

"It's freezing in here." Daren stared around at the control bank under the wide windscreen, his bare arms and legs, skin clay-brown from the sun, ridged with goosebumps.

So much bare skin scared Zipakna. Average age for onset of melanoma without regular boosters was twenty-five. "Want something to drink? You can go look at the chickens. They're in the back."

"Water?" The boy gave him a bright, hopeful look. "Ella has a chicken. She lets me take care of it." He disappeared into the chicken space.

Zipakna opened the egg fridge. Bianca laid steadily even though she didn't have the peak capacity that some of the others did. So he had a good stock of her eggs. The boy was murmuring to the hens who were clucking greetings at him. "You can take one out," Zipakna called back to him. "They like to be held." He opened a packet of freeze-dried chocolate soy milk, reconstituted it and whipped one of Bianca's eggs into it, so that it frothed tawny and rich. The gods knew if the boy had ever received any immunizations at all. Bianca provided the basic panel of nanobodies against most of the common pathogens and cancers. Including melanoma.

In the chicken room, Daren had taken Bella out of her cage, held her cradled in his arms. The speckled black and white hen clucked contentedly, occasionally pecking Daren's chin lightly. "She likes to be petted," Zipakna said. "If you rub her comb she'll sing to you. I made you a milkshake."

The boy's smile blossomed as Bella gave out with the almost-melodic squawks and creaks that signified her pleasure. "What's a milkshake?" Still smiling, he returned the hen to her cage and eyed the glass.

"Soymilk and chocolate and sugar." He handed it to Daren, found himself holding his breath as the boy tasted it and considered.

"Pretty sweet." He drank some. "I like it anyway."

To Zipakna's relief he drank it all and licked foam from his lip.

"So when did you move here?" Zipakna took the empty glass rinsed it at the sink.

"Wow, you use water to clean dishes?" The boy's eyes had widened. "We came here last planting time. Pierre brought those seeds." He pointed in the general direction of the sunflower fields.

Zipakna's heart sank. "You and your parents?" He made his voice light.

Daren didn't answer for a moment. "Pierre. My father." He looked back to the chicken room. "If they're not magic, why do you give them water? Ella's chicken warns her about snakes, but you don't have to worry about snakes in here. What good are they?"

The cold logic of the Dry, out here beyond the security net of civilized space. "Their eggs keep you healthy." He watched the boy consider that. "You know Ella, right?" He waited for the boy's nod. "She has a disease that would kill her if she didn't eat an egg from that chicken you were holding every year."

Daren frowned, clearly doubting that. "You mean like a snake egg? They're good, but Ella's chicken doesn't lay eggs. And snake eggs don't make you get better when you're sick."

"They don't. And Ella's chicken is a banty rooster. He doesn't lay eggs." Zipakna looked up as a figure moved on the heads-up. "Bella is special and so are her eggs." He opened the door. "Hello, Ella, what are you doing out here in the heat?"

"I figured he'd be out here bothering you." Ella hoisted herself up the Dragon's steps, her weathered, sun-dried face the color of real leather, her loose sun-shirt falling back from the stringy muscles of her arms as she reached up to kiss Zipakna on the cheek. "You behavin' yourself, boy? I'll switch you if you aren't."

"I'm being good." Daren grinned. "Ask him."

"He is." Zipakna eyed her face and briefly exposed arms, looking for any sign of melanoma. Even with the eggs, you could still get it out here with no UV protection. "So, Ella, you got some new additions to town, eh? New crops, too, I see." He watched her look away, saw her face tighten.

"Now don't you start." She stared at the south viewscreen filled with the bright heads of sunflowers. "Prices on everything we have to buy keep going up. And the Pima are tight, you know that. Plain sunflower oil don't bring much."

"So now you got something that can get you raided. By the government or someone worse."

"You're the one comes out here from the city where you got water and power, go hiking around in the dust with enough stuff to keep raiders fat and happy for a year." Ella's leathery face creased into a smile. "You preachin' risk at me, Zip?"

"Ah, but we know I'm crazy, eh?" He returned her smile, but shook his head. "I hope you're still here, next trip. How're you're sugar levels? You been checking?"

"If we ain't we ain't." She lifted one bony shoulder in a shrug. "They're holding. They always do."

"The eggs do make you well?" Daren looked at Ella.

"Yeah, they do." Ella cocked her head at him. "There's magic, even if Pierre don't believe it."

"Do you really come from a city?" Daren was looking up at Zipakna now. "With a dome and water in the taps and everything?"

"Well, I come from Oaxaca, which doesn't have a dome. I spend most of my time in La Paz. It's on the Baja peninsula, if you know where that is."

"I do." He grinned. "Ella's been schooling me. I know where Oaxaca is, too. You're Mexican, right?" He tilted his head. "How come you come up here with your eggs?"

Ella was watching him, her dark eyes sharp with surmise. Nobody had ever asked him that question openly before. It wasn't the kind of question you asked, out here. Not out loud. He looked down into Daren's hazel eyes, into *her* eyes. "Because nobody else does."

Daren's eyes darkened and he looked down at the floor, frowning slightly.

"Sit down, Ella, let me get you your egg. Long as you're here." Zipakna turned quickly to the kitchen wall and filled glasses with water. While they drank, he got Bella's fresh egg from the egg-fridge and cracked it into a glass, blending it with the raspberry concentrate that Ella favored and a bit of soy milk.

"That's a milkshake," Daren announced as Zipakna handed Ella the glass. "He made me one, too." He looked up at Zipakna. "I'm not sick."

"He didn't think you were." Ella lifted her glass in a salute. "Because nobody else does." Drank it down. "You gonna come eat with us tonight?" Usually the invitation came with a grin that revealed the gap in her upper front teeth, and a threat about her latest pequin salsa. Today her smile was cautious. Wary. "Daren?" She nodded at the boy. "You go help Maria with the food. You know it's your turn today."

"Aw." He scuffed his bare feet, but headed for the door. "Can I come pet the chickens again?" He looked back hopefully from the door, grinned at Zipakna's nod, and slipped out, letting in a breath of oven-air.

"Ah, Ella." Zipakna sighed and reached into the upper cupboard. "Why did you plant those damn sunflowers?" He pulled out the bottle of aged mescal tucked away behind the freeze-dried staples. He filled a small, thick glass and set it down on the table in front of Ella beside her refilled water glass. "This can be the end of the settlement. You know that."

"The end can come in many ways." She picked up the glass, held it up to the light. "Perhaps fast is better than slow, eh?" She sipped the liquor, closed her eyes and sighed. "Luna and her husband tried for amnesty, applied to get a citizen-visa at the border. They've canceled the amnesty. You live outside the serviced areas, I guess you get to stay out here. I guess the US economy faltered again. No more new citizens from Outside. And you know Mexico's policy about US immigration." She shrugged. "I'm surprised they even let you come up here."

"Oh, my government doesn't mind traffic in this direction. It likes to rub the US's nose in the fact that we send aid to its own citizens," he said lightly. Yeah, the border was closed tight to immigration from the north right now, because the US was being sticky about tariffs. "I can't believe they've made the Interior Boundaries airtight." That was what *she* had been afraid of, all those years ago.

"I guess they have to keep cutting and cutting." Ella drained the glass, probing for the last drops of amber liquor with her tongue. "No, one is enough." She shook her head as he turned to the cupboard. "The folks that live nice want to keep it that way, so you got to cut somewhere. We all know the US is slowly eroding away. It's not a superpower anymore. They just pretend." She looked up at Zipakna, her eyes like flakes of obsidian set into the nested wrinkles of her sun-dried face. "What is your interest in the boy, Zip? He's too young."

He turned away from those obsidian flake eyes. "You misunderstand."

She waited, didn't say anything.

"Once upon a time there was a woman." He stared at the sun-baked emptiness of the main street on the vid screen. A tumbleweed skeleton turned slowly, fitfully across dust and cracked asphalt. "She had a promising career in academics, but she preferred field work."

"Field work?"

"She was a botanist. She created some drought tolerant GMOs and started field testing them. They were designed for the drip irrigation ag areas, but she decided to test them . . . out here. She . . . got caught up in it . . . establishing adaptive GMOs out here to create sustainable harvests. She . . . gave up an academic career. Put everything into this project. Got some funding for it."

Ella sat without speaking as the silence stretched between them. "What happened to her?" She asked it, finally.

"I don't know." The tumbleweed had run up against the pole of a rusted and dented *No Parking* sign and quivered in the hot wind. "I . . . lost contact with her."

Ella nodded, her face creased into thoughtful folds. "I see."

No, you don't, he thought.

"How long ago?"

"Fifteen years."

"So he's not your son."

He flinched even though he'd known the question was coming. "No." He was surprised at how hard it was to speak that word.

Ella levered herself to her feet, leaning hard on the table. Pain in her hip. The osteo-sarcoma antibodies Red produced weren't specific to her problem. A personally tailored anti-cancer panel might cure her, but that cost money. A lot of money. He wasn't a doctor, but he'd seen enough osteo out here to measure her progress. It was the water, he guessed. "I brought you a present." He reached up into the cupboard again, brought out a flat plastic bottle of mescal with the Mexico state seal on the cap. Old stuff. Very old.

She took it, her expression enigmatic, tilted it, her eyes on the slosh of pale golden liquor. The she let her breath out in a slow sigh and tucked the bottle carefully beneath her loose shirt. "Thank you." Her obsidian eyes gave nothing away.

He caught a glimpse of rib bones, faint bruising, and dried, shrunken flesh, revised his estimate. "You're welcome."

"I think you need to leave here." She looked past him. "We maybe need to live without your eggs. I'd just go right now."

He didn't answer for a moment. Listened to the chuckle of the hens. "Can I come to dinner tonight?"

"That's right. You're crazy. We both know that." She sighed.

He held the door for her as she lowered herself stiffly and cautiously into the oven heat of the fading day.

She was right, he thought as he watched her limp through the heat shimmer, back to the main building. She was definitely right.

He took his time with the chickens, letting them out of their cages to scratch on the grass carpet and peck at the vitamin crumbles he scattered for them. While he was parked here, they could roam loose in the back of the Dragon. He kept the door leading back to their section locked and all his hens were good about laying in their own cages, although at this point, he could tell who had laid which egg by sight. By the time he left the Dragon, the sun was completely down and the first pale stars winked in the royal blue of the darkening sky. No moon tonight. The wind had died and he smelled dust and a whiff of roasting meat as his boots grated on the dusty asphalt of the old main street. He touched the small hardness of the stunner in his pocket and climbed the sagging porch of what had once been a store, back when the town had still lived.

They had built a patio of sorts out behind the building, had roofed it from the sun with metal sheeting stripped from other derelict buildings. Long tables and old sofas clustered inside the building, shelter from the sun on the long hot days where residents shelled sunflower seed after harvest or worked on repair jobs or just visited, waiting for the cool of evening. He could see the yellow flicker of flame out back through the old, plate-glass windows with their taped cracks.

The moment he entered he felt it—tension like the prickle of static electricity on a dry, windy day. Paloma was easy, friendly. He let his guard down sometimes when he was here, sat around the fire pit out back and shared the mescal he brought, trading swallows with the local stuff, flavored with cactus fruit, that wasn't all that bad, considering.

Tonight, eyes slid his way, slid aside. The hair prickled on the back of his neck, but he made his smile easy. "Hola," he said, and gave them the usual grin and wave. "How you all makin' out?"

"Zip." Ella heaved herself up from one of the sofas, crossed the floor with firm strides, hands out, face turning up to kiss his cheeks. Grim determination folded the skin at the corners of her eyes tight. "Glad you could eat with us. Thanks for that egg today, I feel better already."

Ah, that was the issue? "Got to keep that blood sugar low." He gave her a real hug, because she was so *solid*, was the core of this settlement, whether the others realized it or not.

"Come on." Ella grabbed his arm. "Let's go out back. Rodriguez got an antelope, can you believe it? A young buck, no harm done."

"Meat?" He laughed, made it relaxed and easy, from the belly. "You eat better than I do. It's all vat stuff or too pricey to afford, down south. Good thing maize and beans are in my blood."

"Hey." Daren popped in from the firelit back, his eyes bright in the dim light. "Can my friends come see the chickens?"

My friends. The shy, hopeful pride in those words was so naked that Zipakna almost winced. He could see two or three faces behind Daren. That same tone had tainted his own voice, back when he had been a government scholarship kid from the wilds beyond San Cristobal, one of those who spoke Spanish as a second language. *My friends*, such a precious thing when you did not belong.

"Sure." He gave Daren a 'we're buddies' grin and shrug. "Any time. You can show 'em around." Daren's eyes betrayed his struggle to look nonchalant.

A low chuckle circulated through the room, almost too soft to be heard and Ella touched his arm lightly. Approvingly. Zipakna felt the tension relax a bit as he and Ella made their way through the dusk of the building to the firelit dark out back. One by one the shadowy figures who had stood back, not greeted him, thawed and followed. He answered greetings, pretending he hadn't noticed anything, exchanged the usual pleasantries that concerned weather and world politics, avoided the real issues of life. Like illegal crops. One by one, he identified the faces as the warm red glow of the coals in the firepit lit them. She needed the MS egg from Negro, he needed the anti-malaria from Seca and so did she. Daren had appeared at his side, his posture taut, a mix of proprietary and anxious.

"Meat, what a treat, eh?" Zipakna grinned down at Daren as one of the women laid a charred strip of roasted meat on a plate, dumped a scoop of beans beside it and added a flat disk of tortilla, thick and chewy and gritty from the bicycle powered stone-mill that the community used to grind maize into masa.

"Hey, you be careful tomorrow." She ndded toward a plastic bucket filled with water, a dipper and cups beside it. "Don't you let my Jonathan hurt any of those chickens. He's so clumsy."

"I'll show 'em how to be careful." Daren took the piled plate she handed him, practically glowing with pride.

Zipakna smiled at the server. She was another diabetic, like Ella. Sanja. He remembered her name.

"Watch out for the chutney." Sanja grinned and pointed at a table full of condiment dishes. "The sticky red stuff. I told Ella how to make it and she made us all sweat this year with her pequins."

"I like it hot." He smiled for her. "I want to see if it'll make me sweat."

"It will." Daren giggled. "I thought I'd swallowed coals, man." He carried his plate to one of the wooden tables, set it down with a possessive confidence beside Zipakna's.

Usually he sat at a crowded table answering questions, sharing news that hadn't yet filtered out here with the few traders, truckers, or wanderers who risked the unserviced Dry. Not this time. He chewed the charred, overdone meat slowly, aware of the way Daren wolfed his food, how most of the people here ate the same way, always prodded by hunger. That was how they drank, too, urgently, always thirsty.

Not many of them meant to end up out there. He remembered her words, the small twin lines that he called her 'thinking dimples' creasing her forehead as she stared into her wine glass. *They had plans, they had a future in mind. It wasn't this one.*

"That isn't really why you come out here, is it? What you said before— in your big truck?"

Zipakna started, realized he was staring into space, a forkful of beans poised in the air. He looked down at Daren, into those clear hazel eyes that squeezed his heart. She had always known when he wasn't telling the truth. "No. It isn't." He set the fork down on his plate. "A friend of mine . . . a long time ago . . . went missing out here. I've . . . sort of hoped to run into her." At least that was how it had started. Now he looked for her ghost. Daren was staring at his neck.

"Where did you get that necklace?"

Zipakna touched the carved jade cylinder on its linen cord. "I found it diving in an old cenote—that's a kind of well where people threw offerings to the gods centuries ago. You're not supposed to dive there, but I was a kid—sneaking in."

"Are the cenotes around here?" Daren looked doubtful. "I never heard of any wells."

"No, they're way down south. Where I come from."

Daren scraped up the last beans from his plate, wiped it carefully with his tortilla. "Why did your friend come out here?"

"To bring people plants that didn't need much water." Zipakna sighed and eyed the remnants of his dinner. "You want this? I'm not real hungry tonight."

Daren gave him another doubting look, then shrugged and dug into the last of the meat and beans. "She was like Pierre?"

"No!"

The boy flinched and Ziapkna softened his tone. "She created food plants so that you didn't need to grow as much to eat well." And then . . . she had simply gotten too involved. He closed his eyes, remembering that bitter, bitter fight. "Is your mother here?" He already knew the answer but Daren's head shake still pierced him. The boy focused on wiping up the last molecule of the searing sauce with a scrap of tortilla, shoulders hunched.

"What are you doing?"

At the angry words, Daren's head shot up and he jerked his hands away from the plate as if it had burned him.

"I was just talking with him, Pierre." He looked up, sandy hair falling back form his face. "He doesn't mind."

"I mind." The tall, skinny man with the dark braid and pale skin frowned down at Daren. "What have I told you about city folk?"

"But . . . " Daren bit off the word, ducked his head. "I'll go clean my plate." He snatched his plate and cup from the table, headed for the deeper shadows along the building.

"You leave him alone." The man stared down at him, his gray eyes flat and cold. "We all know about city folk and their appetites."

Suddenly the congenial chatter that had started up during the meal, ended. Silence hung thick as smoke in the air. "You satisfied my appetite quite well tonight." Zipakna smiled gently. "I haven't had barbecued antelope in a long time."

"You got to wonder." Pierre leaned one hip against the table, crossed his arms. "Why someone gives up the nice air conditioning and swimming pools of the city to come trekking around out here handing out free stuff. Especially when your rig costs a couple of fortunes."

Zipakna sighed, made it audible. From the corner of his eye he noticed Ella, watching him intently, was aware of the hard lump of the stunner in his pocket. "I get this every time I meet folk. We already went through it here, didn't anyone tell you?"

"Yeah, they did." Pierre gave him a mirthless smile. "And you want me to believe that some non-profit in Mexico—Mexico!—cares about us? Not even our own government does that."

"It's all politics." Zipakna shrugged. "Mexico takes quite a bit of civic pleasure in rubbing the US's nose in the fact that Mexico has to extend aid to US citizens. If the political situation changes, yeah, the money might dry up. But for now, people contribute and I come out here. So do a few others like me." He looked up, met the man's cold, gray eyes. "Haven't you met an altruist at least once in your life?" he asked softly.

Pierre looked away and his face tightened briefly. "I sure don't believe you're one. You leave my son alone." He turned on his heel and disappeared in the direction Daren had taken.

Zipakna drank his water, skin prickling with the feel of the room. He looked up as Ella marched over, sat down beside him. "We know you're what you say you are." She pitched her voice to reach everyone. "Me, I'm looking forward to my egg in the morning, and I sure thank you for keeping an old woman like me alive. Not many care. He's right about that much." She gave Zipakna a small private wink as she squeezed his shoulder and stood up. "Sanja and I'll be there first thing in the morning, right, Sanja?"

"Yeah." Sanja's voice emerged from shadow, a little too bright. "We sure will."

Zipakna got to his feet and Ella rose with him. "You should all come by in the morning. Got a new virus northwest of here. It's high mortality and it's moving this way. Spread by birds, so it'll get here. I have eggs that will give you immunity." He turned and headed around the side of the building.

A thin scatter of replies drifted after him and he found Ella walking beside him, her hand on his arm. "They change everything," she said softly. "The flowers."

"You know, the sat cams can see them." He kept his voice low as they crunched around the side of the building , heading toward the Dragon. "They measure the light refraction from the leaves and they can tell if they're legit or one of the outlaw strains. That's no accident, Ella. You don't realize how much the government and the drug gangs use the same tools. One or the other will get you." He shook his head. "You better hope it's the government."

"They haven't found us yet."

"The seeds aren't ready to harvest are they?"

"Pierre says we're too isolated."

Zipakna turned on her. "Nowhere is isolated any more. Not on this entire dirt ball. You ever ask Pierre why he showed up here? Why didn't he stay where he was before if he was doing such a good job growing illegal seeds?"

Ella didn't answer and he walked on.

"It's a mistake to let a ghost run your life." Ella's voice came low from the darkness behind him, tinged with sadness.

Zipakna hesitated as the door slid open for him. "Good night, Ella." He climbed into its cool interior, listening to the hens' soft chortle of greeting.

They showed up in the cool of dawn, trickling up to the Dragon in ones and twos to drink the frothy blend of fruit and soymilk he offered and to ask shyly about the news they hadn't asked about last night. A few apologized. Not many.

Neither Daren nor Pierre showed up. Zipakna fed the hens, collected the day's eggs and was glad he'd given Daren his immunization egg the day before. By noon he had run out of things to keep him here. He hiked over to the community building in the searing heat of noon, found Ella sewing a shirt in the still heat of the interior, told her goodbye.

"Go with God," she told him and her face was as seamed and dry as the land outside.

This settlement would not be here when he next came this way. The old gods wrote that truth in the dust devils dancing at the edge of the field.

He wondered what stolen genes those seeds carried. He looked for Daren and Pierre but didn't see either of them. Tired to the bone, he trudged back to the Dragon in the searing heat. Time to move on. Put kilometers between the Dragon and the dangerous magnet of those ripening seeds.

You have a visitor, the Dragon announced as he approached.

He hadn't locked the door? Zipakna frowned, because he didn't make that kind of mistake. Glad that he was still carrying the stunner, he slipped to the side and opened the door, fingers curled around the smooth shape of the weapon.

"Ella said you were leaving." Daren stood inside, Bella in his arms.

"Yeah, I need to move on." He climbed up, the wash of adrenalin through his bloodstream telling him just how tense it had been here. "I have other settlements to visit."

Daren looked up at him, frowning a little. Then he turned and went back into the chicken room to put Bella back in her traveling coop. He scratched her comb, smiled a little as she chuckled at him, and closed the door. "I think maybe . . . this is yours." He turned and held out a hand.

Zipakna stared down at the carved jade cylinder on his palm. It had been strung on a fine steel chain. She had worn it on a linen cord with coral beads knotted on either side of it. He swallowed. Shook his head. "It's yours." The words came out husky and rough. "She meant you to have it."

"I thought maybe she was the friend you talked about." Daren closed his fist around the bead. "She said the same thing you did, I remember. She said she came out here because no one else would. Did you give it to her?"

He nodded, squeezing his eyes closed, struggling to swallow the pain that welled up into his throat. "You can come with me," he whispered. "You're her son. Did she tell you she had dual citizenship—for both the US and Mexico? You can get citizenship in Mexico. Your DNA will prove that you're her son."

"I'd have to ask Pierre." Daren looked up at him, his eyes clear, filled with a maturity far greater than his years. "He won't say yes. He doesn't like the cities and he doesn't like Mexico even more."

Zipakna clenched his teeth, holding back the words that he wanted to use to describe Pierre. Lock the door, he thought. Just leave. Make Daren understand as they rolled on to the next settlement. "What happened to her?" he said softly, so softly.

"A border patrol shot her." Daren fixed his eyes on Bella who was fussing and clucking in her cage. "A chopper. They were just flying over, shooting coyotes. They shot her and me."

She had a citizen chip. If they'd had their scanner on, they would have picked up the signal. He closed his eyes, his head filled with roaring. Yahoos out messing around, who was ever gonna check up? Who cared? When he opened his eyes, Daren was gone, the door whispering closed behind him.

What did any of it matter? He blinked dry eyes and went forward to make sure the thermosolar plant was powered up. It was. He released the brakes and pulled into a tight turn, heading southward out of town on the old, cracked asphalt of the dead road.

He picked up the radio chatter in the afternoon as he fed the hens and let the unfurled panels recharge the storage batteries. He always listened, had paid a lot of personal money for the top decryption chip every trek. He wanted to know who was talking out here and about what.

US border patrol. He listened with half an ear as he scraped droppings from the crate pans and dumped them into the recycler. He knew the acronyms, you mostly got US patrols out here. *Flower-town.* It came over in a sharp, tenor voice. He straightened, chicken shit spilling from the dustpan in his hand as he listened. Hard.

Paloma. What else could 'Flower-town' be out here? They were going to hit it. Zipakna stared down at the scattered gray and white turds on the floor. Stiffly, slowly, he knelt and brushed them into the dust pan. This was the only outcome. He knew it. Ella knew it. They'd made the choice. *Not many of them meant to end up out there.* Her voice murmured in his ear, so damn earnest. *They had plans, they had a future in mind. It wasn't this one.*

"Shut up!" He bolted to his feet, flung the pan at the wall. "Why did you have his kid?" The pan hit the wall and shit scattered everywhere. The hens panicked, squawking and beating at the mesh of their crates. Zipakna dropped to his knees, heels of his hands digging into his eyes until red light webbed his vision.

Flower-town. It came in over the radio, thin and wispy now, like a ghost voice.

Zipakna stumbled to his feet, went forward and furled the solar panels. Powered up and did a tight 180 that made the hens squawk all over again.

The sun sank over the rim of the world, streaking the ochre ground with long, dark shadows that pointed like accusing fingers. He saw the smoke in the last glow of the day, mushrooming up in a black flag of doom. He switched the Dragon to infrared navigation, and the black and gray images popped up on the heads-up above the console. He was close. He slowed his speed, wiped sweating palms on his shirt. They'd have a perimeter alarm set and they'd pick him up any minute now. If they could claim he was attacking them, they'd blow him into dust in a heartbeat. He'd run into US government patrols out here before and they didn't like the Mexican presence one bit. But his movements were sat-recorded and recoverable and Mexico would love to accuse the US of firing on one of its charity missions in the world media. So he was safe. If he was careful. He slowed the Dragon even more although he wanted to race. Not that there would be much he could do.

He saw the flames first and the screen darkened as the nightvision program filtered the glare. The community building? More flames sprang to life in the sunflower fields.

Attention Mexican registry vehicle N45YG90. The crudely accented Spanish filled the Dragon. *You are entering an interdicted area. Police action is in progress and no entry is permitted.*

Zipakna activated his automatic reply. "I'm sorry. I will stop here. I have a faulty storage bank and I'm almost out of power. I won't be able to go any farther until I can use my panels in the morning." He sweated in the silence, the hens clucking softly in the rear.

Stay in your vehicle. The voice betrayed no emotion. *Any activity will be viewed as a hostile act. Understand?*

"Of course." Zipakna broke the connection. The air in the Dragon seemed syrupy thick, pressing against his ear drums. They could be scanning him, watching to make sure that he didn't leave the Dragon. All they needed was an excuse. He heard a flurry of sharp reports. Gunshots. He looked up at the screen, saw three quick flashes of light erupt from the building beyond the burning community center. No, they'd be looking there. Not here.

Numbly he stood and pulled his protective vest from its storage cubicle along with a pair of night goggles. He put the Dragon on standby. Just in case. If he didn't reactivate it in forty-eight hours, it would send a mayday back to headquarters. They'd come and collect the hens and the Dragon. He looked once around the small, dimly lit space of the Dragon, said a prayer to the old gods and touched the jade at his throat. Then he touched the door open, letting in a dry breath of desert that smelled of bitter smoke, and slipped out into the darkness.

He crouched, moving with the fits and starts of the desert coyotes, praying again to the old gods that the patrol wasn't really worrying about him. Enough clumps of mesquite survived here in this long ago wash to give him some visual cover from anyone looking in his direction and as he remembered, the wash curved north and east around the far end of the old town. It would take him close to the outermost buildings.

It seemed to take a hundred years to reach the tumble down shack that marked the edge of the town. He slipped into its deeper shadow. A half moon had risen and his goggles made the landscape stand out in bright black and gray and white. The gunfire had stopped. He slipped from shed to the fallen ruins of an old house, to the back of an empty storefront across from the community building. It was fully in flames now and his goggles damped the light as he peered cautiously from the glassless front window. Figures moved in the street, dressed in military coveralls. They had herded a dozen people together at the end of the street and Zipakna saw the squat, boxy shapes of two big military choppers beyond them.

They would not have a good future, would become permanent residents of a secure resettlement camp somewhere. He touched his goggles, his stomach lurching as he zoomed in on the bedraggled settlers. He recognized Sanja, didn't see either Ella or Daren, but he couldn't make out too many faces in the huddle. If the patrol had them, there was nothing he could do. They were searching the buildings on this side of the street. He saw helmeted figures cross the street, heading for the building next to his vantage point.

Zipakna slipped out the back door, made his way to the next building, leaned through the sagging window opening. "Daren? Ella? It's Zip," he said softly. "Anyone there?" Silence. He didn't dare raise his voice, moved on to the next building, his skin tight, expecting a shouted command. If they caught him interfering they'd arrest him. It might be a long time before Mexico got him freed. His bosses would be very unhappy with him.

"Ella?" He hurried, scrabbling low through fallen siding, tangles of old junk. They weren't here. The patrol must have made a clean sweep. He felt a brief, bitter stab of satisfaction that they had at least caught Pierre. One would deserve his fate, anyway.

Time to get back to the Dragon. As he turned, he saw two shadows slip into the building he had just checked—one tall, one child short. Hope leaped in his chest, nearly choking him. He bent low and sprinted, trying to gauge the time . . . how long before the patrol soldiers got to this building? He reached a side window, its frame buckled. As he did, a slight figure scrambled over the broken sill and even in the black and white of nightvision, Zipakna recognized Daren's fair hair.

The old gods had heard him. He grabbed the boy, hand going over his mouth in time to stifle his cry. "It's me. Zip. Be silent," he hissed.

Light flared in the building Daren had just left. Zipakna's goggles filtered it and crouching in the dark, clutching Daren, he saw Pierre stand up straight, hands going into the air. "All right, I give up. You got me." Two uniformed patrol pointed stunners at Pierre.

Daren's whimper was almost but not quite soundless. "Don't move," Zipakna breathed. If they hadn't seen Daren . . .

"You're the one brought the seeds." The taller of the two lowered his stunner and pulled an automatic from a black holster on his hip. "We got an ID on you."

A gun? Zipakna stared at it as it rose in seeming slow motion, the muzzle tracking upward to Pierre's stunned face. Daren lunged in his grip and he yanked the boy down and back, hurling him to the ground. The stunner seemed to have leaped from his pocket to his hand and the tiny dart hit the man with the gun smack in the center of his chest. A projectile vest didn't stop a stunner charge. The man's arms spasmed outward and the ugly automatic went sailing, clattering to the floor. Pierre dived for the window as the other patrol yanked out his own weapon and pointed it at Zipakna. He fired a second stun charge but as he did, something slammed into his shoulder and threw him backward. Distantly he heard a loud noise, then Daren was trying to drag him to his feet.

"Let's go." Pierre yanked him upright.

"This way." Zipakna pointed to the distant bulk of the Dragon.

They ran. His left side was numb but there was no time to think about that. Daren and Pierre didn't have goggles so they ran behind him. He took them through the mesquite, ignoring the thorn slash, praying that the patrol focused on the building first before they started scanning the desert. His back twitched with the expectation of a bullet.

The Dragon opened to him and he herded them in, gasping for breath now, the numbness draining away, leaving slow, spreading pain in its wake. "In here." He touched the hidden panel and it opened, revealing the coffin shaped space beneath the floor. The Dragon was defended, but this was always the backup. Not even a scan could pick up someone hidden here. "You'll have to both fit. There's air." They managed it, Pierre clasping Daren close, the boy's face buried against his shoulder. Pierre looked up as the panel slid closed. "Thanks." The panel clicked into place.

Zipakna stripped off his protective vest. Blood soaked his shirt. They were using piercers. That really bothered him, but fortunately the vest had slowed the bullet enough. He slapped a blood-stop patch onto the injury, waves of pain washing through his head, making him dizzy. Did a stim-tab from the med closet and instantly straightened, pain and dizziness blasted away by the drug. Didn't dare hide the bloody shirt, so he pulled a loose woven shirt over his head. *Visitor*, the Dragon announced. *US Security ID verified.*

"Open." Zipakna leaned a hip against the console, aware of the heads-up that still showed the town. The building had collapsed into a pile of glowing embers and dark figures darted through the shadows. "Come in." He said it in English with a careful US accent. "You're really having quite a night over there." He stood back as two uniformed Patrol burst into the Dragon while a third watched warily from the doorway. All carrying stunners.

Not guns, so maybe, just maybe, they hadn't been spotted.

"What are you up to?" The Patrol in charge, a woman, stared at him coldly through the helmet shield. "Did you leave this vehicle or let anyone in?"

The gods had come through. Maybe. "Goodness, no." He arched his eyebrows. "I'm not that crazy. I'm still stunned that Paloma went to raising pharm." He didn't have to fake the bitterness. "That's why you're burning the fields, right? They're a good bunch of people. I didn't think they'd ever give in to that."

Maybe she heard the truth in his words, but for whatever reason, the leader relaxed a hair. "Mind if we look around?" It wasn't a question and he shrugged, stifling a wince at the pain that made it through the stimulant buzz.

"Sure. Don't scare the hens, okay?"

The two inside the Dragon searched, quickly and thoroughly. They checked to see if he had been recording video and Zipakna said thanks to the old gods that he hadn't activated it. That would have changed things, he was willing to bet.

"You need help with your battery problem?" The cold faced woman ... a lieutenant, he noticed her insignia ... asked him.

He shook his head. "I'm getting by fine as long as I don't travel at night. They store enough for life support."

"I'd get out of here as soon as the sun is up." She jerked her head at the other two. "Any time you got illegal flowers you get raiders. You don't want to mess with them."

"Yes, ma'am." He ducked his head. "I sure will do that." He didn't move as they left, waited a half hour longer just to be sure that they didn't pop back in. But they did not. Apparently they believed his story, hadn't seen their wild dash through the mesquite. He set the perimeter alert to maximum and opened the secret panel. Daren scrambled out first, his face pale enough that his freckles stood out like bits of copper on his skin.

Her freckles.

Zipakna sat down fast. When the stim ran out, you crashed hard. The room tilted, steadied.

"That guy shot you." Daren's eyes seemed to be all pupil. "Are you going to die?"

"You got medical stuff?" Pierre's face swam into view. "Tell me quick, okay?"

"The cupboard to the left of the console." The words came out thick. Daren was staring at his chest. Zipakna looked down. Red was soaking into the ivory weave of the shirt he'd put on. So much for the blood-stop. The bullet must have gone deeper than he thought, or had hit a small artery. Good thing his boarders hadn't stuck around longer.

Pierre had the med kit. Zipakna started to pull the shirt off over his head and the pain hit him like a lightning strike, sheeting his vision with white. He saw the pale green arch of the ceiling, thought *I'm falling . . .*

He woke in his bed, groping drowsily for where he was headed and what he had drunk that made his head hurt this bad. Blinked as a face swam into view. Daren. He pushed himself up to a sitting position, his head splitting.

"You passed out." Daren's eyes were opaque. "Pierre took the bullet out of your shoulder while you were out. You bled a lot but he said you won't die."

"Where's Pierre?" He swung his legs over the side of the narrow bed, fighting dizziness. "How long have I been out?"

"Not very long." Daren backed away. "The chickens are okay. I looked."

"Thanks." Zipakna made it to his feet, steadied himself with a hand on the wall. A quick check of the console said that Pierre hadn't messed with anything. It was light out. Early morning. He set the video to sweep, scanned the landscape. No choppers, no trace of last night's raiders. He watched the images pan across the heads-up; blackened fields, the smoldering pile of embers and twisted plumbing that had been the community center, still wisping smoke. The fire had spread to a couple of derelict building to the windward of the old store. Movement snagged his eye. Pierre. Digging. He slapped the control, shut off the vid. Daren was back with the chickens. "Stay here, okay? I'm afraid to leave them alone."

"Okay." Daren's voice came to him, hollow as an empty egg shell.

He stepped out into the oven heat, his head throbbing in time to his footsteps as he crossed the sunbaked ground to the empty bones of

Paloma. A red bandanna had snagged on a mesquite branch, flapping in the morning's hot wind. He saw a woman's sandal lying on the dusty asphalt of the main street, a faded red backpack. He picked it up, looked inside. Empty. He dropped it, crossed the street, angling northward to where he had seen Pierre digging.

He had just about finished two graves. A man lay beside one. The blood that soaked his chest had turned dark in the morning heat. Zipakna recognized his grizzled red beard and thinning hair, couldn't remember his name. He didn't eat any of the special eggs, just the ones against whatever new bug was out there. Pierre climbed out of the shallow grave.

"You shouldn't be walking around." He pushed dirty hair out of his eyes.

Without a word, Zipakna moved to the man's ankles. Pierre shrugged, took the man's shoulders. He was stiff, his flesh plastic and too cold, never mind the morning heat. Without a word they lifted and swung together, lowered him into the fresh grave. It probably wouldn't keep the coyotes out, Zipakna thought. But it would slow them down. He straightened, stepped over to the other grave.

Ella. Her face looked sad, eyes closed. He didn't see any blood, wondered if she had simply suffered a heart attack, if she had had enough as everything she had worked to keep intact burned around her. "Did Daren see her die?" He said it softly. Felt rather than saw Pierre's flinch.

"I don't know. I don't think so." He stuck the shovel into the piled rocks and dirt, tossed the first shovel full into the hole.

Zipakna said the right words in rhythm to the grating thrust of the shovel. First the Catholic prayer his mother would have wanted him to say, then the words for the old gods. Then a small, hard prayer for the new gods who had no language except dust and thirst and the ebb and flow of world politics that swept human beings from the chess board of the earth like pawns.

"You could have let them shoot me." Pierre tossed a last shovel full of dirt onto Ella's grave. "Why didn't you?"

Zipakna tilted his gaze to the hard blue sky. "Daren." Three tiny black specks hung overhead. Vultures. Death called them. "I'll make you a trade. I'll capitalize you to set up as a trader out here. You leave the pharm crops alone. I take Daren with me and get him Mexican citizenship. Give him a future better than yours."

"You can't." Pierre's voice was low and bitter. "I tried. Even though his mother was a US citizen, they're not taking in offspring born out here. Mexico has a fifteen year waiting list for new immigrants." He was staring down at the mounded rock and dust of Ella's grave. "She was so angry when she got pregnant. The implant was faulty, I guess. She meant to go back to the city before he was born but . . . I got hurt. And she stuck around." He was silent for awhile. "Then it was too late, Daren was born and the US had closed the border. We're officially out here because we want to be." His lips twisted.

"Why did you come out here?"

He looked up. Blinked. "My parents lived out here. They were the rugged individual types, I guess." He shrugged. "I went into the city, got a job, and they were still letting people come and go then. I didn't like it, all the people, all the restrictions. So I came back out here." He gave a thin laugh. "I was a trader to start with. I got hit by a bunch of raiders. That's when . . . I got hurt. Badly. I'm sorry." He turned away. "I wish you could get him citizenship. He didn't choose this."

"I can." Zipakna watched Pierre halt without turning. "She . . . was my wife. We married in Oaxaca." The words were so damn hard to say. "That gave her automatic dual citizenship. In Mexico, only the mother's DNA is required as proof of citizenship. We're pragmatists," he said bitterly.

For a time, Pierre said nothing. Finally he turned, his face as empty as the landscape. "You're the one." He looked past Zipakna, toward the Dragon. "I don't like you, you know. But I think . . . you'll be a good father for Daren. Better than I've been." He looked down at the dirty steel of the shovel blade. "It's a deal. A trade. I'll sell you my kid. Because it's a good deal for him." He walked past Zipakna toward the Dragon, tossed the shovel into the narrow strip of shade along one of the remaining buildings. The clang and rattle as it hit sounded loud as mountain thunder in the quiet of the windless heat.

Zipakna followed slowly, his shoulder hurting. Ilena would be pissed, would never believe that Daren wasn't his. His mouth crooked with the irony of that. The old gods twisted time and lives into the intricate knots of the universe and you could meet yourself coming around any corner. As the Dragon's doorway opened with a breath of cool air, he heard Pierre's voice from the chicken room, low and intense against the cluck and chortle of the hens, heard Daren's answer, heard the brightness in it.

Zipakna went forward to the console to ready the Dragon for travel. As soon as they reached the serviced lands again he'd transfer his savings to a cash card for Pierre. Pierre could buy what he needed on the Pima's land. They didn't care if you were a Drylander or not.

Ilena would be doubly pissed. But he was a good poker partner and she wouldn't dump him. And she'd like Daren. Once she got past her jealousy. Ilena had always wanted a kid, just never wanted to take the time to *have* one.

He wondered if she had meant to contact him, tell him about Daren, bring the boy back to Mexico. She would have known, surely, that it would have been all right.

Surely. He sighed and furled the solar wings.

Maybe he would keep coming out here. If Daren wanted to. Maybe her ghost would find them as they traveled through this place she had loved. And then he could ask her.

First published in *Asimov's Science Fiction Magazine,* February, 2008.

ABOUT THE AUTHOR

One of the most popular and prolific of the new writers of the '90s, **Mary Rosenblum** made her first sale in 1990, and soon became one of that decade's most prolific contributors at short story lengths, making dozens of sales to many different magazines and anthologies. Her linked series of "Drylands" stories, about an American Southwest rendered uninhabitable by prolonged droughts, now seems, alas, more germane than ever, and was recently collected in an expanded version as *Water Rites.* The original version, *The Drylands,* won the prestigious Compton Crook Award for Best First Novel of the year in 1993. Her other books include the SF novels *Chimera, The Stone Garden,* and *Horizons,* and a short story collection, *Synthesis and Other Stories.* She has also written a trilogy of mystery novels written under the name Mary Freeman. Rosenblum won the Sidewise Award for Alternate History in 2009 for her story "Sacrifice." A graduate of Clarion West, Mary Rosenblum lives in Canby, Oregon, and runs the website New Writers Interface. Her most recent book is *Self Publishing Success: A Handbook for New Writers.*

Mountain Ways

URSULA K. LE GUIN

Note for readers unfamiliar with the planet O:
Ki'O society is divided into two halves or moieties, called (for ancient religious reasons) the Morning and the Evening. You belong to your mother's moiety, and you can't have sex with anybody of your moiety.

Marriage on O is a foursome, the sedoretu—a man and a woman from the Morning moiety and a man and a woman from the Evening moiety. You're expected to have sex with both your spouses of the other moiety, and not to have sex with your spouse of your own moiety. So each sedoretu has two expected heterosexual relationships, two expected homosexual relationships, and two forbidden heterosexual relationships.

The expected relationships within each sedoretu are:
The Morning woman and the Evening man (the "Morning marriage")
The Evening woman and the Morning man (the "Evening marriage")
The Morning woman and the Evening woman (the "Day marriage")
The Morning man and the Evening man (the "Night marriage")
The forbidden relationships are between the Morning woman and the Morning man, and between the Evening woman and the Evening man, and they aren't called anything, except sacrilege.

It's just as complicated as it sounds, but aren't most marriages?

In the stony uplands of the Deka Mountains the farmholds are few and far between. Farmers scrape a living out of that cold earth, planting on sheltered slopes facing south, combing the yama for fleece, carding and spinning and weaving the prime wool, selling pelts to the carpet-factories. The mountain yama, called ariu, are a small wiry breed; they run wild, without shelter, and are not fenced in, since they never cross the invisible, immemorial boundaries of the herd territory. Each farmhold is in fact a herd territory. The animals are the true farmholders. Tolerant

69

and aloof, they allow the farmers to comb out their thick fleeces, to assist them in difficult births, and to skin them when they die. The farmers are dependent on the ariu; the ariu are not dependent on the farmers. The question of ownership is moot. At Danro Farmhold they don't say, "We have nine hundred ariu," they say, "The herd has nine hundred."

Danro is the farthest farm of Oro Village in the High Watershed of the Mane River on Oniasu on O. The people up there in the mountains are civilised but not very civilised. Like most ki'O they pride themselves on doing things the way they've always been done, but in fact they are a wilful, stubborn lot who change the rules to suit themselves and then say the people "down there" don't know the rules, don't honor the old ways, the true ki'O ways, the mountain ways.

Some years ago, the First Sedoretu of Danro was broken by a landslide up on the Farren that killed the Morning woman and her husband. The widowed Evening couple, who had both married in from other farmholds, fell into a habit of mourning and grew old early, letting the daughter of the Morning manage the farm and all its business.

Her name was Shahes. At thirty, she was a straight-backed, strong, short woman with rough red cheeks, a mountaineer's long stride, and a mountaineer's deep lungs. She could walk down the road to the village center in deep snow with a sixty-pound pack of pelts on her back, sell the pelts, pay her taxes and visit a bit at the village hearth, and stride back up the steep zigzags to be home before nightfall, forty kilometers round trip and six hundred meters of altitude each way. If she or anyone else at Danro wanted to see a new face they had to go down the mountain to other farms or to the village center. There was nothing to bring anybody up the hard road to Danro. Shahes seldom hired help, and the family wasn't sociable. Their hospitality, like their road, had grown stony through lack of use.

But a traveling scholar from the lowlands who came up the Mane all the way to Oro was not daunted by another near-vertical stretch of ruts and rubble. Having visited the other farms, the scholar climbed on around the Farren from Ked'din and up to Danro, and there made the honorable and traditional offer: to share worship at the house shrine, to lead conversation about the Discussions, to instruct the children of the farmhold in spiritual matters, for as long as the farmers wished to lodge and keep her.

This scholar was an Evening woman, over forty, tall and long-limbed, with cropped dark-brown hair as fine and curly as a yama's. She was quite fearless, expected nothing in the way of luxury or even comfort, and had no small talk at all. She was not one of the subtle and eloquent expounders of the great Centers. She was a farm woman who had gone to school. She read and talked about the Discussions in a plain way that suited her hearers, sang the offerings and the praise songs to the oldest tunes, and gave brief, undemanding lessons to Danro's one child, a ten-year-old Morning half-nephew. Otherwise she was as silent as her hosts, and as hardworking. They were up at dawn; she was up before dawn to sit in meditation. She studied her few books and wrote for an hour or two after that. The rest of the day she worked alongside the farm people at whatever job they gave her.

It was fleecing season, midsummer, and the people were all out every day, all over the vast mountain territory of the herd, following the scattered groups, combing the animals when they lay down to chew the cud.

The old ariu knew and liked the combing. They lay with their legs folded under them or stood still for it, leaning into the comb-strokes a little, sometimes making a small, shivering whisper-cough of enjoyment. The yearlings, whose fleece was the finest and brought the best price raw or woven, were ticklish and frisky; they sidled, bit, and bolted. Fleecing yearlings called for a profound and resolute patience. To this the young ariu would at last respond, growing quiet and even drowsing as the long, fine teeth of the comb bit in and stroked through, over and over again, in the rhythm of the comber's soft monotonous tune, "Hunna, hunna, na, na . . . . "

The traveling scholar, whose religious name was Enno, showed such a knack for handling new-born eriu that Shahes took her out to try her hand at fleecing yearlings. Enno proved to be as good with them as with the infants, and soon she and Shahes, the best fine-fleecer of Oro, were working daily side by side. After her meditation and reading, Enno would come out and find Shahes on the great slopes where the yearlings still ran with their dams and the new-borns. Together the two women could fill a forty-pound sack a day with the airy, silky, milk-colored clouds of combings. Often they would pick out a pair of twins, of which there had been an unusual number this mild year. If Shahes led out one twin the other would follow it, as yama twins will do all their lives; and so the women could work side by side in a silent, absorbed companionship. They talked only to the animals. "Move your fool leg," Shahes would say to the yearling she was combing, as it gazed at her with its great, dark, dreaming eyes. Enno would murmur "Hunna, hunna, hunna, na," or hum a fragment of an Offering, to soothe her beast when it shook its disdainful, elegant head and showed its teeth at her for tickling its belly. Then for half an hour nothing but the crisp whisper of the combs, the flutter of the unceasing wind over stones, the soft bleat of a calf, the faint rhythmical sound of the nearby beasts biting the thin, dry grass. Always one old female stood watch, the alert head poised on the long neck, the large eyes watching up and down the vast, tilted planes of the mountain from the river miles below to the hanging glaciers miles above. Far peaks of stone and snow stood distinct against the dark-blue, sun-filled sky, blurred off into cloud and blowing mists, then shone out again across the gulfs of air.

Enno took up the big clot of milky fleece she had combed, and Shahes held open the long, loose-woven, double-ended sack.

Enno stuffed the fleece down into the sack. Shahes took her hands.

Leaning across the half-filled sack they held each other's hands, and Shahes said, "I want—" and Enno said, "Yes, yes!"

Neither of them had had much love, neither had had much pleasure in sex. Enno, when she was a rough farm girl named Akal, had the misfortune to attract and be attracted by a man whose pleasure was in cruelty. When she finally understood that she did not have to endure what he did to her, she ran away, not knowing how else to escape him. She took refuge at the School in Asta, and there found the work and learning much to her liking, as she did the spiritual discipline, and later the wandering life. She had been an itinerant scholar with no family, no close attachments, for twenty years. Now Shahes' passion opened to her a spirituality of the body, a revelation that transformed the world and made her feel she had never lived in it before.

As for Shahes, she'd given very little thought to love and not much more to sex, except as it entered into the question of marriage. Marriage was an urgent matter of business. She was thirty years old. Danro had no whole sedoretu, no child-bearing women, and only one child. Her duty was plain. She had gone courting in a grim, reluctant fashion to a couple of neighboring farms where there were Evening men. She was too late for the man at Beha Farm, who ran off with a lowlander. The widower at Upper Ked'd was receptive, but he also was nearly sixty and smelled like piss. She tried to force herself to accept the advances of Uncle Mika's half-cousin from Okro Farm down the river, but his desire to own a share of Danro was clearly the sole substance of his desire for Shahes, and he was even lazier and more shiftless than Uncle Mika.

Ever since they were girls, Shahes had met now and then with Temly, the Evening daughter of the nearest farmhold, Ked'din, round on the other side of the Farren. Temly and Shahes had a sexual friendship that was a true and reliable pleasure to them both. They both wished it could be permanent. Every now and then they talked, lying in Shahes' bed at Danro or Temly's bed at Ked'din, of getting married, making a sedoretu. There was no use going to the village matchmakers; they knew everybody the matchmakers knew. One by one they would name the men of Oro and the very few men they knew from outside the Oro Valley, and one by one they would dismiss them as either impossible or inaccessible. The only name that always stayed on the list was Otorra, a Morning man who worked at the carding sheds down in the village center. Shahes liked his reputation as a steady worker; Temly liked his looks and conversation. He evidently liked Temly's looks and conversation too, and would certainly have come courting her if there were any chance of a marriage at Ked'din, but it was a poor farmhold, and there was the same problem there as at Danro: there wasn't an eligible Evening man. To make a sedoretu, Shahes and Temly and Otorra would have to marry the shiftless, shameless fellow at Okba or the sour old widower at Ked'd. To Shahes the idea of sharing her farm and her bed with either of them was intolerable.

"If I could only meet a man who was a match for me!" she said with bitter energy.

"I wonder if you'd like him if you did," said Temly.

"I don't know that I would."

"Maybe next autumn at Manebo . . . "

Shahes sighed. Every autumn she trekked down sixty kilometers to Manebo Fair with a train of pack-yama laden with pelts and wool, and looked for a man; but those she looked at twice never looked at her once. Even though Danro offered a steady living, nobody wanted to live way up there, on the roof, as they called it. And Shahes had no prettiness or nice ways to interest a man. Hard work, hard weather, and the habit of command had made her tough; solitude had made her shy. She was like a wild animal among the jovial, easy-talking dealers and buyers. Last autumn once more she had gone to the fair and once more strode back up into her mountains, sore and dour, and said to Temly, "I wouldn't touch a one of 'em."

Enno woke in the ringing silence of the mountain night. She saw the small square of the window ablaze with stars and felt Shahes' warm body beside her shake with sobs.

"What is it? what is it, my dear love?"

"You'll go away. You're going to go away!"

"But not now—not soon—"

"You can't stay here. You have a calling. A resp—" the word broken by a gasp and sob—"responsibility to your school, to your work, and

I can't keep you. I can't give you the farm. I haven't anything to give you, anything at all!"

Enno—or Akal, as she had asked Shahes to call her when they were alone, going back to the girl-name she had given up—Akal knew only too well what Shahes meant. It was the farmholder's duty to provide continuity. As Shahes owed life to her ancestors she owed life to her descendants. Akal did not question this; she had grown up on a farmhold. Since then, at school, she had learned about the joys and duties of the soul, and with Shahes she had learned the joys and duties of love. Neither of them in any way invalidated the duty of a farmholder. Shahes need not bear children herself, but she must see to it that Danro had children. If Temly and Otorra made the Evening marriage, Temly would bear the children of Danro. But a sedoretu must have a Morning marriage; Shahes must find an Evening man. Shahes was not free to keep Akal at Danro, nor was Akal justified in staying there, for she was in the way, an irrelevance, ultimately an obstacle, a spoiler. As long as she stayed on as a lover, she was neglecting her religious obligations while compromising Shahes' obligation to her farmhold. Shahes had said the truth: she had to go.

She got out of bed and went over to the window. Cold as it was she stood there naked in the starlight, gazing at the stars that flared and dazzled from the far grey slopes up to the zenith. She had to go and she could not go. Life was here, life was Shahes' body, her breasts, her mouth, her breath. She had found life and she could not go down to death. She could not go and she had to go.

Shahes said across the dark room, "Marry me."

Akal came back to the bed, her bare feet silent on the bare floor. She slipped under the bedfleece, shivering, feeling Shahes' warmth against her, and turned to her to hold her; but Shahes took her hand in a strong grip and said again, "Marry me."

"Oh if I could!"

"You can."

After a moment Akal sighed and stretched out, her hands behind her head on the pillow. "There's no Evening men here; you've said so yourself. So how can we marry? What can I do? Go fishing for a husband down in the lowlands, I suppose. With the farmhold as bait. What kind of man would that turn up? Nobody I'd let share you with me for a moment. I won't do it."

Shahes was following her own train of thought. "I can't leave Temly in the lurch," she said.

"And that's the other obstacle," Akal said. "It's not fair to Temly. If we do find an Evening man, then she'll get left out."

"No, she won't."

"Two Day marriages and no Morning marriage? Two Evening women in one sedoretu? There's a fine notion!"

"Listen," Shahes said, still not listening. She sat up with the bedfleece round her shoulders and spoke low and quick. "You go away. Back down there. The winter goes by. Late in the spring, people come up the Mane looking for summer work. A man comes to Oro and says, is anybody asking for a good finefleecer? At the sheds they tell him, yes, Shahes from Danro was down here looking for a hand. So he comes on up here, he knocks at the door here. My name is Akal, he says, I hear you need a fleecer. Yes, I say, yes, we do. Come in. Oh come in, come in and stay forever!"

Her hand was like iron on Akal's wrist, and her voice shook with exultation. Akal listened as to a fairytale.

"Who's to know, Akal? Who'd ever know you? You're taller than most men up here—you can grow your hair, and dress like a man—you said you liked men's clothes once. Nobody will know. Who ever comes here anyway?"

"Oh, come on, Shahes! The people here, Magel and Madu—Shest—"

"The old people won't see anything. Mika's a halfwit. The child won't know. Temly can bring old Barres from Ked'din to marry us. He never knew a tit from a toe anyhow. But he can say the marriage ceremony."

"And Temly?" Akal said, laughing but disturbed; the idea was so wild and Shahes was so serious about it.

"Don't worry about Temly. She'd do anything to get out of Ked'din. She wants to come here, she and I have wanted to marry for years. Now we can. All we need is a Morning man for her. She likes Otorra well enough. And he'd like a share of Danro."

"No doubt, but he gets a share of me with it, you know! A woman in a Night marriage?"

"He doesn't have to know."

"You're crazy, of course he'll know!"

"Only after we're married."

Akal stared through the dark at Shahes, speechless. Finally she said, "What you're proposing is that I go away now and come back after half a year dressed as a man. And marry you and Temly and a man I never met. And live here the rest of my life pretending to be a man. And nobody is going to guess who I am or see through it or object to it. Least of all my husband."

"He doesn't matter."

"Yes he does," said Akal. "It's wicked and unfair. It would desecrate the marriage sacrament. And anyway it wouldn't work. I couldn't fool everybody! Certainly not for the rest of my life!"

"What other way have we to marry?"

"Find an Evening husband—somewhere—"

"But I want you! I want you for my husband and my wife. I don't want any man, ever. I want you, only you till the end of life, and nobody between us, and nobody to part us. Akal, think, think about it, maybe it's against religion, but who does it hurt? Why is it unfair? Temly likes men, and she'll have Otorra. He'll have her, and Danro. And Danro will have their children. And I will have you, I'll have you forever and ever, my soul, my life and soul."

"Oh don't, oh don't," Akal said with a great sob.

Shahes held her.

"I never was much good at being a woman," Akal said. "Till I met you. You can't make me into a man now! I'd be even worse at that, no good at all!"

"You won't be a man, you'll be my Akal, my love, and nothing and nobody will ever come between us."

They rocked back and forth together, laughing and crying, with the fleece around them and the stars blazing at them. "We'll do it, we'll do it!" Shahes said, and Akal said, "We're crazy, we're crazy!"

Gossips in Oro had begun to ask if that scholar woman was going to spend the winter up in the high farmholds, where was she now, Danro was it or Ked'din?—when she came walking down the zigzag road. She spent the night and sang the offerings for the mayor's family, and caught the daily freighter to the suntrain station down at Dermane. The first of the autumn blizzards followed her down from the peaks.

Shahes and Akal sent no message to each other all through the winter. In the early spring Akal telephoned the farm. "When are you coming?" Shahes asked, and the distant voice replied, "In time for the fleecing."

For Shahes the winter passed in a long dream of Akal. Her voice sounded in the empty next room. Her tall body moved beside Shahes through the wind and snow. Shahes' sleep was peaceful, rocked in a certainty of love known and love to come.

For Akal, or Enno as she became again in the lowlands, the winter passed in a long misery of guilt and indecision. Marriage was a sacrament, and surely what they planned was a mockery of that sacrament. Yet as surely it was a marriage of love. And as Shahes had said, it harmed no one—unless to deceive them was to harm them. It could not be right to fool the man, Otorra, into a marriage where his Night partner would turn out to be a woman. But surely no man knowing the scheme beforehand would agree to it; deception was the only means at hand. They must cheat him.

The religion of the ki'O lacks priests and pundits who tell the common folk what to do. The common folk have to make their own moral and spiritual choices, which is why they spend a good deal of time discussing the Discussions. As a scholar of the Discussions, Enno knew more questions than most people, but fewer answers.

She sat all the dark winter mornings wrestling with her soul. When she called Shahes, it was to tell her that she could not come. When she heard Shahes' voice her misery and guilt ceased to exist, were gone, as a dream is gone on waking. She said, "I'll be there in time for the fleecing."

In the spring, while she worked with a crew rebuilding and repainting a wing of her old school at Asta, she let her hair grow. When it was long enough, she clubbed it back, as men often did. In the summer, having saved a little money working for the school, she bought men's clothes. She put them on and looked at herself in the mirror in the shop. She saw Akal. Akal was a tall, thin man with a thin face, a bony nose, and a slow, brilliant smile. She liked him.

Akal got off the High Deka freighter at its last stop, Oro, went to the village center, and asked if anybody was looking for a fleecer.

"Danro."—"The farmer was down from Danro, twice already."— "Wants a finefleecer."—"Coarsefleecer, wasn't it?"—It took a while, but the elders and gossips agreed at last: a finefleecer was wanted at Danro.

"Where's Danro?" asked the tall man.

"Up," said an elder succinctly. "You ever handled ariu yearlings?"

"Yes," said the tall man. "Up west or up east?"

They told him the road to Danro, and he went off up the zigzags, whistling a familiar praise-song.

As Akal went on he stopped whistling, and stopped being a man, and wondered how she could pretend not to know anybody in the household, and how she could imagine they wouldn't know her. How could she deceive Shest, the child whom she had taught the water rite and the praise-songs? A pang of fear and dismay and shame shook her when she saw Shest come running to the gate to let the stranger in.

Akal spoke little, keeping her voice down in her chest, not meeting the child's eyes. She was sure he recognised her. But his stare was simply that of a child who saw strangers so seldom that for all he knew they all looked alike. He ran in to fetch the old people, Magel and Madu. They came out to offer Akal the customary hospitality, a religious duty, and Akal accepted, feeling mean and low at deceiving these people, who had always been kind to her in their rusty, stingy way, and at the same time feeling a wild impulse of laughter, of triumph. They did not see Enno in her, they did not know her. That meant that she was Akal, and Akal was free.

She was sitting in the kitchen drinking a thin and sour soup of summer greens when Shahes came in—grim, stocky, weatherbeaten, wet. A summer thunderstorm had broken over the Farren soon after Akal reached the farm. "Who's that?" said Shahes, doffing her wet coat.

"Come up from the village." Old Magel lowered his voice to address Shahes confidentially: "He said they said you said you wanted a hand with the yearlings."

"Where've you worked?" Shahes demanded, her back turned, as she ladled herself a bowl of soup.

Akal had no life history, at least not a recent one. She groped a long time. No one took any notice, prompt answers and quick talk being unusual and suspect practices in the mountains. At least she said the name of the farm she had run away from twenty years ago. "Bredde Hold, of Abba Village, on the Oriso."

"And you've finefleeced? Handled yearlings? Ariu yearlings?"

Akal nodded, dumb. Was it possible that Shahes did not recognise her? Her voice was flat and unfriendly, and the one glance she had given Akal was dismissive. She had sat down with her soupbowl and was eating hungrily.

"You can come out with me this afternoon and I'll see how you work," Shahes said. "What's your name, then?"

"Akal."

Shahes grunted and went on eating. She glanced up across the table at Akal again, one flick of the eyes, like a stab of light.

Out on the high hills, in the mud of rain and snowmelt, in the stinging wind and the flashing sunlight, they held each other so tight neither could breathe, they laughed and wept and talked and kissed and coupled in a rock shelter, and came back so dirty and with such a sorry little sack of combings that old Magel told Madu that he couldn't understand why Shahes was going to hire the tall fellow from down there at all, if that's all the work was in him, and Madu said what's more he eats for six.

But after a month or so, when Shahes and Akal weren't hiding the fact that they slept together, and Shahes began to talk about making a sedoretu, the old couple grudgingly approved. They had no other kind of approval to give. Maybe Akal was ignorant, didn't know a hassel-bit from a cold-chisel; but they were all like that down there. Remember that travelling scholar, Enno, stayed here last year, she was just the same, too tall for her own good and ignorant, but willing to learn, same as Akal. Akal was a prime hand with the beasts, or had the makings of it anyhow. Shahes could look farther and do worse. And it meant she and and Temly could be the Day marriage of a sedoretu, as they would have been long since if there'd been any kind of men around worth taking into the farmhold, what's wrong with this generation, plenty of good men around in my day.

Shahes had spoken to the village matchmakers down in Oro. They spoke to Otorra, now a foreman at the carding sheds; he accepted a formal invitation to Danro. Such invitations included meals and an overnight stay, necessarily, in such a remote place, but the invitation was to share worship with the farm family at the house shrine, and its significance was known to all.

So they all gathered at the house shrine, which at Danro was a low, cold, inner room walled with stone, with a floor of earth and stones that was the unlevelled ground of the mountainside. A tiny spring, rising at the higher end of the room, trickled in a channel of cut granite. It was the reason why the house stood where it did, and had stood there for six hundred years. They offered water and accepted water, one to another, one from another, the old Evening couple, Uncle Mika, his son Shest, Asbi who had worked as a pack-trainer and handyman at Danro for thirty years, Akal the new hand, Shahes the farmholder, and the guests: Otorra from Oro and Temly from Ked'din.

Temly smiled across the spring at Otorra, but he did not meet her eyes, or anyone else's.

Temly was a short, stocky woman, the same type as Shahes, but fairer-skinned and a bit lighter all round, not as solid, not as hard. She had a surprising, clear singing voice that soared up in the praise-songs. Otorra was also rather short and broad-shouldered, with good features, a competent-looking man, but just now extremely ill at ease; he looked as if he had robbed the shrine or murdered the mayor, Akal thought, studying him with interest, as well she might. He looked furtive; he looked guilty.

Akal observed him with curiosity and dispassion. She would share water with Otorra, but not guilt. As soon as she had seen Shahes, touched Shahes, all her scruples and moral anxieties had dropped away, as if they could not breathe up here in the mountains. Akal had been born for Shahes and Shahes for Akal; that was all there was to it. Whatever made it possible for them to be together was right.

Once or twice she did ask herself, what if I'd been born into the Morning instead of the Evening moiety?—a perverse and terrible thought. But perversity and sacrilege were not asked of her. All she had to do was change sex. And that only in appearance, in public. With Shahes she was a woman, and more truly a woman and herself than she had ever been in her life. With everybody else she was Akal, whom they took to be a man. That was no trouble at all. She was Akal; she liked being Akal. It was not like acting a part. She never had been herself with other people, had always felt a falsity in her relationships with them; she had never known who she was at all, except sometimes for a moment in meditation, when her *I am* became *It is,* and she breathed the stars. But with Shahes she was herself utterly, in time and in the body, Akal, a soul consumed in love and blessed by intimacy.

So it was that she had agreed with Shahes that they should say nothing to Otorra, nothing even to Temly. "Let's see what Temly makes of you," Shahes said, and Akal agreed.

Last year Temly had entertained the scholar Enno overnight at her farmhold for instruction and worship, and had met her two or three times at Danro. When she came to share worship today she met Akal for the first time. Did she see Enno? She gave no sign of it. She greeted Akal with a kind of brusque goodwill, and they talked about breeding ariu. She quite evidently studied the newcomer, judging, sizing up; but that was natural enough in a woman meeting a stranger she might be going to marry. "You don't know much about mountain farming, do you?" she said kindly after they had talked a while. "Different from down there. What did you raise? Those big flatland yama?" And Akal told her about the farm where she grew up, and the three crops a year they got, which made Temly nod in amazement.

As for Otorra, Shahes and Akal colluded to deceive him without ever saying a word more about it to each other. Akal's mind shied away from the subject. They would get to know each other during the engagement period, she thought vaguely. She would have to tell him, eventually, that she did not want to have sex with him, of course, and the only way to do that without insulting and humiliating him was to say that she, that Akal, was averse to having sex with other men, and hoped he would forgive her. But Shahes had made it clear that she mustn't tell him that till they were married. If he knew it beforehand he would refuse to enter the sedoretu. And even worse, he might talk about it, expose Akal as a woman, in revenge. Then they would never be able to marry. When Shahes had spoken about this Akal had felt distressed and trapped, anxious, guilty again; but

Shahes was serenely confident and untroubled, and somehow Akal's guilty feelings would not stick. They dropped off. She simply hadn't thought much about it. She watched Otorra now with sympathy and curiosity, wondering what made him look so hangdog. He was scared of something, she thought.

After the water was poured and the blessing said, Shahes read from the Fourth Discussion; she closed the old boxbook very carefully, put it on its shelf and its cloth over it, and then, speaking to Magel and Madu as was proper, they being what was left of the First Sedoretu of Danro, she said, "My Othermother and my Otherfather, I propose that a new sedoretu be made in this house."

Madu nudged Magel. He fidgeted and grimaced and muttered inaudibly. Finally Madu said in her weak, resigned voice, "Daughter of the Morning, tell us the marriages."

"If all be well and willing, the marriage of the Morning will be Shahes and Akal, and the marriage of the Evening will be Temly and Otorra, and the marriage of the Day will be Shahes and Temly, and the marriage of the Night will be Akal and Otorra."

There was a long pause. Magel hunched his shoulders. Madu said at last, rather fretfully, "Well, is that all right with everybody?"—which gave the gist, if not the glory, of the formal request for consent, usually couched in antique and ornate language.

"Yes," said Shahes, clearly.

"Yes," said Akal, manfully.

"Yes," said Temly, cheerfully.

A pause.

Everybody looked at Otorra, of course. He had blushed purple and, as they watched, turned greyish.

"I am willing," he said at last in a forced mumble, and cleared his throat. "Only—" He stuck there.

Nobody said anything.

The silence was horribly painful.

Akal finally said, "We don't have to decide now. We can talk. And, and come back to the shrine later, if . . . "

"Yes," Otorra said, glancing at Akal with a look in which so much emotion was compressed that she could not read it at all—terror, hate, gratitude, despair?—"I want to—I need to talk—to Akal."

"I'd like to get to know my brother of the Evening too," said Temly in her clear voice.

"Yes, that's it, yes, that is—" Otorra stuck again, and blushed again. He was in such an agony of discomfort that Akal said, "Let's go on outside for a bit, then," and led Otorra out into the yard, while the others went to the kitchen.

Akal knew Otorra had seen through her pretense. She was dismayed, and dreaded what he might say; but he had not made a scene, he had not humiliated her before the others, and she was grateful to him for that.

"This is what it is," Otorra said in a stiff, forced voice, coming to a stop at the gate. "It's the Night marriage." He came to a stop there, too.

Akal nodded. Reluctantly, she spoke, to help Otorra do what he had to do. "You don't have to—" she began, but he was speaking again:

"The Night marriage. Us. You and me. See, I don't—There's some—See, with men, I—"

The whine of delusion and the buzz of incredulity kept Akal from hearing what the man was trying to tell her. He had to stammer on even more painfully before she began to listen. When his words came clear to her she could not trust them, but she had to. He had stopped trying to talk.

Very hesitantly, she said, "Well, I . . . I was going to tell you . . . . The only man I ever had sex with, it was . . . It wasn't good. He made me—He did things—I don't know what was wrong. But I never have—I have never had any sex with men. Since that. I can't. I can't make myself want to."

"Neither can I," Otorra said.

They stood side by side leaning on the gate, contemplating the miracle, the simple truth.

"I just only ever want women," Otorra said in a shaking voice.

"A lot of people are like that," Akal said.

"They are?"

She was touched and grieved by his humility. Was it men's boastfulness with other men, or the hardness of the mountain people, that had burdened him with this ignorance, this shame?

"Yes," she said. "Everywhere I've been. There's quite a lot of men who only want sex with women. And women who only want sex with men. And the other way round, too. Most people want both, but there's always some who don't. It's like the two ends of," she was about to say "a spectrum," but it wasn't the language of Akal the fleecer or Otorra the carder, and with the adroitness of the old teacher she substituted "a sack. If you pack it right, most of the fleece is in the middle. But there's some at both ends where you tie off, too. That's us. There's not as many of us. But there's nothing wrong with us." As she said this last it did not sound like what a man would say to a man. But it was said; and Otorra did not seem to think it peculiar, though he did not look entirely convinced. He pondered. He had a pleasant face, blunt, unguarded, now that his unhappy secret was out. He was only about thirty, younger than she had expected.

"But in a marriage," he said. "It's different from just . . . A marriage is—Well, if I don't—and you don't—"

"Marriage isn't just sex," Akal said, but said it in Enno's voice, Enno the scholar discussing questions of ethics, and Akal cringed.

"A lot of it is," said Otorra, reasonably.

"All right," Akal said in a consciously deeper, slower voice. "But if I don't want it with you and you don't want it with me why can't we have a good marriage?" It came out so improbable and so banal at the same time that she nearly broke into a fit of laughter. Controlling herself, she thought, rather shocked, that Otorra was laughing at her, until she realised that he was crying.

"I never could tell anybody," he said.

"We don't ever have to," she said. She put her arm around his shoulders without thinking about it at all. He wiped his eyes with his fists like a child, cleared his throat, and stood thinking. Obviously he was thinking about what she had just said.

"Think," she said, also thinking about it, "how lucky we are!"

"Yes. Yes, we are." He hesitated. "But . . . but is it religious . . . to marry each other knowing . . . Without really meaning to . . . . " He stuck again.

After a long time, Akal said, in a voice as soft and nearly as deep as his, "I don't know."

She had withdrawn her comforting, patronising arm from his shoulders. She leaned her hands on the top bar of the gate. She looked at her hands, long and strong, hardened and dirt-engrained from farm work, though the oil of the fleeces kept them supple. A farmer's hands. She had given up the religious life for love's sake and never looked back. But now she was ashamed.

She wanted to tell this honest man the truth, to be worthy of his honesty.

But it would do no good, unless not to make the sedoretu was the only good.

"I don't know," she said again. "I think what matters is if we try to give each other love and honor. However we do that, that's how we do it. That's how we're married. The marriage—the religion is in the love, in the honoring."

"I wish there was somebody to ask," Otorra said, unsatisfied. "Like that travelling scholar that was here last summer. Somebody who knows about religion."

Akal was silent.

83

"I guess the thing is to do your best," Otorra said after a while. It sounded sententious, but he added, plainly, "I would do that."

"So would I," Akal said.

A mountain farmhouse like Danro is a dark, damp, bare, grim place to live in, sparsely furnished, with no luxuries except the warmth of the big kitchen and the splendid bedfleeces. But it offers privacy, which may be the greatest luxury of all, though the ki'O consider it a necessity. "A three-room sedoretu" is a common expression in Okets, meaning an enterprise doomed to fail.

At Danro, everyone had their own room and bathroom. The two old members of the First Sedoretu, and Uncle Mika and his child, had rooms in the center and west wing; Asbi, when he wasn't sleeping out on the mountain, had a cozy, dirty nest behind the kitchen. The new Second Sedoretu had the whole east side of the house. Temly chose a little attic room, up a half-flight of stairs from the others, with a fine view. Shahes kept her room, and Akal hers, adjoining; and Otorra chose the southeast corner, the sunniest room in the house.

The conduct of a new sedoretu is to some extent, and wisely, prescribed by custom and sanctioned by religion. The first night after the ceremony of marriage belongs to the Morning and Evening couples; the second night to the Day and Night couples. Thereafter the four spouses may join as and when they please, but always and only by invitation given and accepted, and the arrangements are to be known to all four. Four souls and bodies and all the years of their four lives to come are in the balance in each of those decisions and invitations; passion, negative and positive, must find its channels, and trust must be established, lest the whole structure fail to found itself solidly, or destroy itself in selfishness and jealousy and grief.

Akal knew all the customs and sanctions, and she insisted that they be followed to the letter. Her wedding night with Shahes was tender and a little tense. Her wedding night with Otorra was also tender; they sat in his room and talked softly, shy with each other but each very grateful; then Otorra slept in the deep windowseat, insisting that Akal have the bed.

Within a few weeks Akal knew that Shahes was more intent on having her way, on having Akal as her partner, than on maintaining any kind of sexual balance or even a pretense of it. As far as Shahes was concerned, Otorra and Temly could look after each other and that was that. Akal had of course known many sedoretu where one or two of the partnerships dominated the others completely, through passion or the power of an ego. To balance all four relationships perfectly was an ideal seldom realised. But this sedoretu, already built on a deception, a disguise, was more fragile than most. Shahes wanted what she wanted and consequences be damned. Akal had followed her far up the mountain, but would not follow her over a precipice.

It was a clear autumn night, the window full of stars, like that night last year when Shahes had said, "Marry me."

"You have to give Temly tomorrow night," Akal repeated.

"She's got Otorra," Shahes repeated.

"She wants you. Why do you think she married you?"

"She's got what she wants. I hope she gets pregnant soon," Shahes said, stretching luxuriously, and running her hand over Akal's breasts and belly. Akal stopped her hand and held it.

"It isn't fair, Shahes. It isn't right."

"A fine one you are to talk!"

"But Otorra doesn't want me, you know that. And Temly does want you. And we owe it to her."

"Owe her what?"

"Love and honor."

"She's got what she wanted," Shahes said, and freed her hand from Akal's grasp with a harsh twist. "Don't preach at me."

"I'm going back to my room," Akal said, slipping lithely from the bed and stalking naked through the starry dark. "Good night."

She was with Temly in the old dye room, unused for years until Temly, an expert dyer, came to the farm. Weavers down in the Centers would pay well for fleece dyed the true Deka red. Her skill had been Temly's dowry. Akal was her assistant and apprentice now.

"Eighteen minutes. Timer set?"

"Set."

Temly nodded, checked the vents on the great dye-boiler, checked the read-out again, and went outside to catch the morning sun. Akal joined her on the stone bench by the stone doorway. The smell of the vegetable dye, pungent and acid-sweet, clung to them, and their clothes and hands and arms were raddled pink and crimson.

Akal had become attached to Temly very soon, finding her reliably good-tempered and unexpectedly thoughtful—both qualities that had been in rather short supply at Danro. Without knowing it, Akal had formed her expectation of the mountain people on Shahes—powerful, wilful, undeviating, rough. Temly was strong and quite self-contained, but open to impressions as Shahes was not. Relationships within her moiety meant little to Shahes; she called Otorra brother because it was customary, but did not see a brother in him. Temly called Akal brother and meant it, and Akal, who had had no family for so long, welcomed the relationship, returning Temly's warmth. They talked easily together, though Akal had constantly to guard herself from becoming too easy and letting her woman-self speak out. Mostly it was no trouble at all being Akal and she gave little thought to it, but sometimes with Temly it was very hard to keep up the pretense, to prevent herself from saying what a woman would say to her sister. In general she had found that the main drawback in being a man was that conversations were less interesting.

They talked about the next step in the dyeing process, and then Temly said, looking off over the low stone wall of the yard to the huge purple slant of the Farren, "You know Enno, don't you?"

The question seemed innocent and Akal almost answered automatically with some kind of deceit—"The scholar that was here . . . ?"

But there was no reason why Akal the fleecer should know Enno the scholar. And Temly had not asked, Do you remember Enno, or did you know Enno, but, "You know Enno, don't you?" She knew the answer.

"Yes."

Temly nodded, smiling a little. She said nothing more.

Akal was amazed by her subtlety, her restraint. There was no difficulty in honoring so honorable a woman.

"I lived alone for a long time," Akal said. "Even on the farm where I grew up I was mostly alone. I never had a sister. I'm glad to have one at last."

"So am I," said Temly.

Their eyes met briefly, a flicker of recognition, a glance planting trust deep and silent as a tree-root.

"She knows who I am, Shahes."

Shahes said nothing, trudging up the steep slope.

"Now I wonder if she knew from the start. From the first water-sharing. . . . "

"Ask her if you like," Shahes said, indifferent.

"I can't. The deceiver has no right to ask for the truth."

"Humbug!" Shahes said, turning on her, halting her in midstride. They were up on the Farren looking for an old beast that Asbi had reported missing from the herd. The keen autumn wind had blown Shahes' cheeks red, and as she stood staring up at Akal she squinted her watering eyes so that they glinted like knifeblades. "Quit preaching! Is that who you are? 'The deceiver?' I thought you were my wife!"

"I am, and Otorra's too, and you're Temly's—you can't leave them out, Shahes!"

"Are they complaining?"

"Do you want them to complain?" Akal shouted, losing her temper. "Is that the kind of marriage you want?—Look, there she is," she added in a suddenly quiet voice, pointing up the great rocky mountainside. Farsighted, led by a bird's circling, she had caught the movement of the yama's head near an outcrop of boulders. The quarrel was postponed. They both set off at a cautious trot towards the boulders.

The old yama had broken a leg in a slip from the rocks. She lay neatly collected, though the broken foreleg would not double under her white breast but stuck out forward, and her whole body had a lurch to that side. Her disdainful head was erect on the long neck, and she gazed at the women, watching her death approach, with clear, unfathomable, uninterested eyes.

"Is she in pain?" Akal asked, daunted by that great serenity.

"Of course," Shahes said, sitting down several paces away from the yama to sharpen her knife on its emery-stone. "Wouldn't you be?"

She took a long time getting the knife as sharp as she could get it, patiently retesting and rewhetting the blade. At last she tested it again and then sat completely still. She stood up quietly, walked over to the yama, pressed its head up against her breast and cut its throat in one long fast slash. Blood leaped out in a brilliant arc. Shahes slowly lowered the head with its gazing eyes down to the ground.

Akal found that she was speaking the words of the ceremony for the dead, *Now all that was owed is repaid and all that was owned, returned. Now all that was lost is found and all that was bound, free.* Shahes stood silent, listening till the end.

Then came the work of skinning. They would leave the carcase to be cleaned by the scavengers of the mountain; it was a carrion-bird circling over the yama that had first caught Akal's eye, and there were now three of them riding the wind. Skinning was fussy, dirty work, in the stink of meat and blood. Akal was inexpert, clumsy, cutting the hide more than once. In penance she insisted on carrying the pelt, rolled as best they could and strapped with their belts. She felt like a grave robber, carrying away the white-and-dun fleece, leaving the thin, broken corpse sprawled among the rocks in the indignity of its nakedness. Yet in her mind as she lugged the heavy fleece along was Shahes standing up and taking the yama's beautiful head against her breast and slashing its throat, all one long movement, in which the woman and the animal were utterly one.

It is need that answers need, Akal thought, as it is question that answers question. The pelt reeked of death and dung. Her hands were caked with blood, and ached, gripping the stiff belt, as she followed Shahes down the steep rocky path homeward.

"I'm going down to the village," Otorra said, getting up from the breakfast table.

"When are you going to card those four sacks?" Shahes said.

He ignored her, carrying his dishes to the washer-rack. "Any errands?" he asked of them all.

"Everybody done?" Madu asked, and took the cheese out to the pantry.

"No use going into town till you can take the carded fleece," said Shahes.

Otorra turned to her, stared at her, and said, "I'll card it when I choose and take it when I choose and I don't take orders at my own work, will you understand that?"

Stop, stop now! Akal cried silently, for Shahes, stunned by the uprising of the meek, was listening to him. But he went on, firing grievance with grievance, blazing out in recriminations. "You can't give all the orders, we're your sedoretu, we're your household, not a lot of hired hands, yes it's your farm but it's ours too, you married us, you can't make all the decisions, and you can't have it all your way either," and at this point Shahes unhurriedly walked out of the room.

"Shahes!" Akal called after her, loud and imperative. Though Otorra's outburst was undignified it was completely justified, and his anger was both real and dangerous. He was a man who had been used, and he knew it. As he had let himself be used and had colluded in that misuse, so now his anger threatened destruction. Shahes could not run away from it.

She did not come back. Madu had wisely disappeared. Akal told Shest to run out and see to the pack-beasts' feed and water.

The three remaining in the kitchen sat or stood silent. Temly looked at Otorra. He looked at Akal.

"You're right," Akal said to him.

He gave a kind of satisfied snarl. He looked handsome in his anger, flushed and reckless. "Damn right I'm right. I've let this go on for too long. Just because she owned the farmhold—"

"And managed it since she was fourteen," Akal cut in. "You think she can quit managing just like that? She's always run things here. She had to. She never had anybody to share power with. Everybody has to learn how to be married."

"That's right," Otorra flashed back, "and a marriage isn't two pairs. It's four pairs!"

That brought Akal up short. Instinctively she looked to Temly for help. Temly was sitting, quiet as usual, her elbows on the table, gathering up crumbs with one hand and pushing them into a little pyramid.

"Temly and me, you and Shahes, Evening and Morning, fine," Otorra said. "What about Temly and her? What about you and me?"

Akal was now completely at a loss. "I thought... When we talked..."

"I said I didn't like sex with men," said Otorra.

She looked up and saw a gleam in his eye. Spite? Triumph? Laughter?

"Yes. You did," Akal said after a long pause. "And I said the same thing."

Another pause.

"It's a religious duty," Otorra said.

Enno suddenly said very loudly in Akal's voice, "Don't come onto me with your religious duty! I studied religious duty for twenty years and where did it get me? Here! With you! In this mess!"

At this, Temly made a strange noise and put her face in her hands. Akal thought she had burst into tears, and then saw she was laughing, the painful, helpless, jolting laugh of a person who hasn't had much practice at it.

"There's nothing to laugh about," Otorra said fiercely, but then had no more to say; his anger had blown up leaving nothing but smoke. He groped for words for a while longer. He looked at Temly, who was indeed in tears now, tears of laughter. He made a despairing gesture. He sat down beside Temly and said, "I suppose it is funny if you look at it. It's just that I feel like a chump." He laughed, ruefully, and then, looking up at Akal, he laughed genuinely. "Who's the biggest chump?" he asked her.

"Not you," she said. "How long...."

"How long do you think?"

It was what Shahes, standing in the passageway, heard: their laughter. The three of them laughing. She listened to it with dismay, fear, shame, and terrible envy. She hated them for laughing. She wanted to be with them, she wanted to laugh with them, she wanted to silence them. Akal, Akal was laughing at her.

She went out to the workshed and stood in the dark behind the door and tried to cry and did not know how. She had not cried when her parents were killed; there had been too much to do. She thought the others were laughing at her for loving Akal, for wanting her, for needing her. She thought Akal was laughing at her for being such a fool, for loving her. She thought Akal would sleep with the man and they would laugh together at her. She drew her knife and tested its edge. She had made it very sharp yesterday on the Farren to kill the yama. She came back to the house, to the kitchen.

They were all still there. Shest had come back and was pestering Otorra to take him into town and Otorra was saying, "Maybe, maybe," in his soft lazy voice.

Temly looked up, and Akal looked round at Shahes—the small head on the graceful neck, the clear eyes gazing.

Nobody spoke.

"I'll walk down with you, then," Shahes said to Otorra, and sheathed her knife. She looked at the women and the child. "We might as well all go," she said sourly. "If you like."

First published in *Asimov's Science Fiction*, August 1996.

ABOUT THE AUTHOR

Ursula K. Le Guin is probably one of the best-known and most universally respected SF writers in the world today, having won, in addition to many Hugo and Nebula Awards, the National Book Award, a Pushcart Prize, The Harold D. Vursell Memorial Award of the American Academy of Arts and Letters, a Newbury Honor, and the World Fantasy Award for Lifetime Achievement. Her famous novel *The Left Hand of Darkness* may have been the most influential SF novel of its decade, and shows every sign of becoming one of the enduring classic of the genre. Le Guin's other novels include *The Dispossessed, Planet of Exile, The Lathe of Heaven, City of Illusions, Rocannon's World, The Beginning Place, A Wizard of Earthsea, The Tombs of Atuan, Tehanu, The Farthest Shore, Searoad,* and *Always Coming Home*. She has had six collections: *The Wind's Twelve Quarters, Orsinian Tales, The Compass Rose, Buffalo Gals and Other Animal Presences, A Fisherman of the Inland Sea,* and *Four Ways to Forgiveness*. She's also written many novels for children as well as much non-fiction. Her most recent books are a novel trilogy, *Gifts, Voices, and Powers,* and two big retrospective collections, *Where On Earth: Selected Stories, Volume One* and *Outer Le Guin, Mountain Ways, 28 Space, Inner Lands: Selected Stories, Volume Two*. She lives with her husband in Portland, Oregon.

A Sympathy of Light and Shadow: Science Fiction, Gothic Horror and How They Met

MARK COLE

The decade started well enough.

We boldly set out into the stars, confident we could conquer every peril. We faced unknown hazards, unexpected consequences of our own actions, beings vastly more powerful than us, and even the darkest corners of our own psyche. Yet we knew the universe would open all its secrets to us.

But then the darkness came. Evil creatures of the night fell upon us. Terrible things stirred in the depths of the earth. Graves burst open, releasing madness, plague and all the monsters of the dead past.

. . . And then the audience bought their popcorn and watched Vincent Price and Christopher Lee, forgetting the aliens, spaceships and distant worlds they'd flocked to see only a few years earlier.

Public taste is notoriously fickle. Nor is it ever easy to explain why it changed. What is certain is that when Hammer films released *The Curse of Frankenstein* in 1957, it proved so successful that other studios rushed to get their own Gothics into the theaters. The fifties SF boom had already peaked—its audience had grown far more discerning, demanding better effects and writing. Many of those who had churned out low budget SF in the Fifties turned to Gothic horror in the Sixties.

It is also clear that these two competing cinematic visions were very different: one bright, clean and evenly-lit; the other shadowy and expressionistic with garish splashes of color: one looking towards the future; the other haunted by the past: one rational even in the face of the unknown; the other feverish and demon-haunted, with madness lurking in the dark.

Which makes it even stranger that a few filmmakers tried to combine the two.

It isn't as if SF hadn't appeared in Gothic fiction before.

Some call *Frankenstein* science fiction, although a lot of people disagree: the novel spends little time on the creation of the monster, focusing instead on its consequences. A few versions put the SF into clearer focus—as in James Whale's bravura 1931 creation scene (suspiciously similar to the demonstrations of real-life "mad scientist" Nicola Tesla) but even his sequel, *The Bride of Frankenstein*, mixes in the supernatural.

Edward Bulwer-Lytton wrote about underground races living in the hollow earth; Jules Verne's one Gothic story throws in a device that records and plays back images; and H.P. Lovecraft's stories offer a more satisfying mix, with ancient aliens, brains in tanks and even fish-men.

Which doesn't change the fact that the mere notion of Gothic SF suggests the mad jumble of clichés in *Plan 9 from Outer Space*.

It was probably inevitable that someone would try to film Lovecraft in an age of Gothic horror films. While he arrived far too late to qualify as Gothic, his stories are filled with enough ancient secrets, crumbling manors and irrational terrors for five Gothic authors. In 1963, Roger Corman made the first attempt with a version of *The Case of Charles Dexter Ward*.

Corman convinced AIP to fund a series of color Edgar Allan Poe movies with higher budgets than they'd given him before (which admittedly wasn't much). The final products, thanks to Corman's gift for working within a tight budget, look very much like the Hammer films he is ripping off.

After making the first five, though, he wanted a break. AIP disagreed: they'd turned their Poe films into a recognizable brand and didn't want to risk making a film by another, lesser-known author. They insisted that he borrow the title of a minor poem, *The Haunted Palace*, and bill it as yet another Poe film (Vincent Price reads a snatch of it at the end, which is Poe's only contribution).

Charles Dexter Ward returns to his ancestral home, Arkham, and finds the town haunted by the monstrous mutations caused by a curse left on it by his ancestor, Joseph Curwen (also Price). Curwen's spirit takes over Ward's body, and takes up where he left off with his experiments with the monstrous creature in a pit under the house. It is a decidedly

Lovecraftian elder god, and there are the expected references to the Necronomicon, Yog-Sothoth and Cthulhu.

Unfortunately, when we finally glimpse the creature, instead of an unspeakable alien monstrosity it looks like the Creature from the Black Lagoon with an extra pair of arms (one suspects a Paul Blaisdell creation leftover from one of Corman's SF films).

Two years later, AIP made the first movie that openly admitted to being a Lovecraft film, *Die, Monster, Die!* Based on *The Colour out of Space*—a rather slight story about a meteor that crashes to earth on a distant farm—it is far more SF than its predecessor. Unfortunately it also has little to do with the original. In the story, the meteor carries a "colour" not part of our spectrum, which corrupts the land around it in an unthinkable way. Here it becomes merely radioactive. An aging Boris Karloff plays a wheelchair-bound scientist who wants to use the power of the meteorite to grow better vegetables. Unfortunately, it has all the usual effects we associate with radiation (well, at least in the movies . . .): killer plants, people reduced to dust, and glowing, axe-wielding maniacs.

Despite its modern setting, the film does manage to create a Gothic mood. Unfortunately, it has little to do with Lovecraft.

Lovecraft has fared poorly in the theaters. The earliest attempts all tried to cram his stories into Corman's Poe framework. Stuart Gordon's 1985 splatter comedy *Re-Animator*, the most successful adaptation to date, broke the formula. It has little in common with his work, however, and was based on a series of short-shorts that Lovecraft himself disdained. Its success, unfortunately, meant that most Lovecraft films after it have been excuses for throwing gore at the screen.

Perhaps the best Lovecraft films to date have been the HPLHS's *The Call of Cthulhu* (2005) and *The Whisperer in Darkness* (2011). While remaining remarkably faithful to the original stories, they offer a heady mix of SF and horror: *The Whisperer in Darkness* even adds an aerial duel between a biplane and a swarm of mechanized alien creatures. However neither film much resembles Hammer's Gothics. Instead they look to the Expressionist silent films, and to King Kong and Universal's horror films from the Forties, respectively, for their inspirations.

By the late Sixties, the Gothic craze was already fading, with a wave of more realistic horrors (like *Rosemary's Baby*) ready to take their place. Hammer responded with more blood and more bare flesh (and a number of oddities, like the first Kung Fu Dracula movie). For some reason, though, despite the great SF films they'd made in the fifties, Hammer never tried adding SF to their Gothic horrors. However, they did bring more than a touch of the Gothic to their version of Nigel Kneale's SF classic, *Quatermass and the Pit* (1967).

The Seventies, however, brought a number of hybrid Gothics, although most of them would be classified as horror rather than true SF. In *The Asphyx* (1972), Sir Hugo Cunningham, a Victorian era scientist fascinated by the question of life after death, has uncovered something strange in the photos of people taken at the moments of their deaths. He believes it to be the Asphyx, a creature from Greek mythology, which carries away the souls of the dying. His experiments uncover a way to trap an Asphyx, which would allow him make people immortal. He then sets out on a series of gruesome experiments, intended to make himself and his family immortal. Of course the results prove catastrophic.

It is a beautifully mounted film that looks and feels like something Hammer might have made. At its heart, it is an inversion of the Frankenstein myth, with the scientific hero trying to unlock not the secrets of life but of death.

In 1973, a team of modern-day scientists and psychics led by physicist Lionel Barrett attempted to conquer the "Mount Everest of haunted houses" in *The Legend of Hell House*, a harrowing film with a script by Richard Mattheson. Barrett has built a machine to end the haunting by eliminating the unfocused electromagnetic force he believes to be the cause of ghostly activity. Not that it works, of course.

It is one of those films that successfully combines a lot of disparate elements, from its Gothic setting to the scientific effort to lay the ghosts, to the sexual tensions within the group. It is intriguing to note that while the preternatural succeeds where rationalism fails, science does seem to have the last word.

Horror Express, a 1972 British/Spanish co-production offered a far more successful blend of Gothic and SF, one that could easily be classed as either. Despite its miniscule budget, poor sound engineering and grainy film, it catches a lot of the spirit of Hammer's horror films, thanks in part to horror icons Christopher Lee and Peter Cushing (and to the set and models borrowed from a more expensive film).

Despite the Victorian setting, the film borrowed heavily from *Quatermass and the Pit*: as in the Hammer classic it is an archaeological dig investigating man's evolutionary origins that releases the alien menace, and the ending where those killed by the body-hopping alien rise up to attack the survivors parallels the madness that overwhelms

London in the earlier film. As in any Quatermass film, it is science that discovers the truth and helps defeat the alien. The images they find floating in an apeman's intraocular fluid are, however, mind-bogglingly absurd.

One might conclude from most of these that the two visions of speculative cinema can only be combined with indifferent results. And yet someone did produce a number of very successful hybrids.

The long running BBC TV series *Doctor Who* had borrowed from Hammer's Quatermass films almost from its beginnings, so it doesn't seem much of a leap for them to look to Hammer's Gothic horror films for inspiration, as in 1971's *The Daemons* which involves a cult and an ancient demonic alien hidden beneath an old church.

But, when Philip Hinchcliffe took over as producer in 1974, he and his script editor, legendary *Who* writer Robert Holmes, deliberately brought Tom Baker's Doctor into the world of the Gothic, both here on Earth and out in the stars, creating some of the show's best serials in the process: "Pyramids of Mars" bears a striking visual resemblance to Hammer's version of *The Mummy* with a healthy dash of Erich von Däniken; "The Brain of Morbius," while set on an alien planet, draws heavily from the more visceral Hammer Frankenstein films (with just a hint of *She*); and the Renaissance setting of "The Masque of Mandragora" calls to mind Corman's Poe films.

The final serial of Hinchcliffe's run, 1977's "The Talons of Weng-Chiang" might best be described as the sort of film Hammer *wanted* to make, with its Victorian Gothic setting and phantasmorgical mixture of period references. It seamlessly combines Sherlock Holmes, Fu Manchu, the Phantom of the Opera, Victorian music halls, giant rats, a time traveling war criminal and a living ventriloquist dummy (leaving Robert Holmes exhausted by the time he finished writing it).

The Gothic still influenced the next season, with "The Horror of Fang Rock," a haunted lighthouse story redolent of William Hope Hodgson's sea stories; and "Image of the Fendahl," which strongly resembles *The Legend of Hell House*, only with a Lovecraftian alien and yet another prehistoric human skull.

However, an unproduced story from the Hinchcliffe era, "State of Decay," resurfaced in 1980. On an alien planet that is a dead ringer for the eastern Europe of Hammer's Dracula movies, the Doctor encounters the last of a monstrous race of space vampires beneath a castle which is really a spaceship.

• • •

One of the better efforts, however, marked Roger Corman's return to directing after an absence of nearly 20 years.

Frankenstein Unbound (1990), based on the novel by Brian Aldiss, starts in the near future, where Dr. Joe Buchanan has developed a weapon which completely obliterates its targets with (supposedly) no harmful effects to anything else. However, a routine test opens up a rift in the time space continuum and Buchanan gets sucked in along with his high-tech car.

He ends up in Switzerland in 1817 where he encounters Mary Shelly not long before she writes *Frankenstein*. But it turns out that Frankenstein is a real person, and his monster is real as well.

Frankenstein Unbound didn't do well at the box office, nor have the critics been kind to it. Which is a shame as it is one of those B-movies which delights in its "B" status, offering both pulpy thrills and a fairly serious exploration of the Frankenstein theme.

By the mid-Seventies Hammer Films was in ruins (although they would continue making TV shows into the Eighties). The Gothic craze died with them.

Despite intermittent attempts to revive it, Gothic horror is still as dead as Frankenstein's bride, with many recent attempts—like *Van Helsing* or *I, Frankenstein*—little more than action films with a little atmosphere. One could argue that it left its mark on some of the darker SF films—certainly *Alien* (1979) has strong parallels to the Gothic, with the wrecked alien ship taking the place of a haunted castle and a more visceral notion of possession and contamination by evil. Don Coscarelli's unclassifiable *Phantasm* (1979) has its share of both SF and Gothic horror but can hardly be said to be either. Or much of anything else anyone ever dreamed up before.

Curiously, the *Warhammer 40,000* RPG—and its cinematic spinoff, *Ultramarines* (2010)—is literally Gothic, with crumbling Gothic fortresses and even spaceships like Gothic cathedrals. One could even note other familiar elements, such as their demonic enemies and the danger of being corrupted by the "warp." But at its heart, *Ultramarines* is a World War II movie writ large.

Perhaps the most promising new film is *Death* (a.k.a., *After Death*) (2012), which has been described as a combination of Gothic horror and Steampunk, although the trailers suggest something rather odder than that.

In film, image is everything. A detailed, well-researched SF world can work well on screen, but it always remains tempting to cheat a little for one perfect image. The visual language a film uses has a great effect on our emotional reaction to what we see on screen, creating mood and atmosphere, and sometimes even acting as a "character" in the story. Most familiar film genres, such as Film Noir or Expressionism are primarily visual categories, whose typical storylines and plots both use and reinforce the genre's visual moods.

Nowhere is this clearer than in some of the better attempts to fuse elements of the Gothic and SF.

It might be tempting to write them off as nothing more than a curiosity, an odd mixture of reason and madness, but the reality is that the Gothic can help explore some of the darker corners of SF. There are stories—often, yes, pulpy, B-movie stories—that cannot be told on screen any other way, dark musings on our own frustrating inability to understand what we still believe to be a rational universe. In particular, Lovecraft demands such treatment.

Whether or not anyone will once again explore the possibilities of Gothic SF is uncertain. One can only hope. In an age when it is easier than ever before for independent film makers to create unique films, perhaps they will once again brave shadows and barely-repressed terrors, ancient curses and horrors from before time to offer us a vision of SF that could not be told any other way.

And you never know: if they hurry, Christopher Lee might still be available.

ABOUT THE AUTHOR

Mark Cole hates writing bios. Despite many efforts he has never written one he likes, perhaps because there are many other things he'd rather be writing. He writes from Warren, Pennsylvania, where he has managed to avoid writing about himself for both newspaper and magazine articles. His musings on Science Fiction have appeared in *Clarkesworld* and at *IROSF.com,* while his most recent story, "(Yet Another Episode of) The BIG Show" ran on *Cosmos Online.*

Beyond the Boundary:
A Conversation with
James L. Cambias

JEREMY L. C. JONES

Above them is ice and around them, the darkling sea. Three cultures—the lobster-like and territorial Ilmatarans, the hyper-sexual and barely constrained Sholen, and the adventurous and somewhat erratic humans—teeter on the brink of conflict.

But this isn't just the story of worlds and cultures, but of individual characters: Rob Freeman, Broadtail, and Tizhos—and, sure, even the unsavory Irona, too.

A Darkling Sea is James L. Cambias' debut novel, but it reads like a thriller penned by a veteran novelist. Indeed, Cambias has been around for a while. He's written extensively for role-playing games and his short stories have been nominated for the Campbell, Nebula, and Tiptree since they started appearing in magazines around 2000.

Regardless of what he's writing, Cambias seems to be enjoying himself thoroughly and that joy pays off for readers. *A Darkling Sea* is a beautifully written, highly suspenseful novel with compelling characters and layers of meaning. It's also a raucous, good-time read.

Below, Cambias and I talk about world-building, characters, and how when you're from Louisiana like he is everything you write is about Louisiana whether you realize it or not.

How much of Louisiana would you say there is in your writing?

I've only written two stories actually set in Louisiana: "The Vampire Brief," in which the comic book hero Hellboy kicks the damned vampire poseurs out of New Orleans, and "See My King All Dressed In Red," in which I flattened my home city with a hurricane.

At this point I probably should say something like " . . . *but really, all my stories are about Louisiana*." Except that I don't think that's true. The part of me that writes science fiction lives in outer space and the far future, and is just as out of place on contemporary Earth as the part of me that lives in New Orleans is out of place in Massachusetts.

If I had to trace any elements of my native state in my work, I think I'd say that growing up in Louisiana taught me very early that institutions are only as good as the people in them, and that self-interested corruption can be less destructive than sincere ideological conviction.

Can you talk about how you built the world of A Darkling Sea—the planet of Ilmatar, the Ilmatarans, the cultures that slam into each other?

Worldbuilding is one of my strengths. In the course of writing two or three different roleplaying game sourcebooks on "how to build a science fiction universe" I've researched the subject pretty exhaustively. All the practical details, like surface gravity, biochemistry, interstellar distances, etc., I can look up or figure out pretty easily. I breathe that stuff now.

So when creating Ilmatar, I could make up a very realistic world that still suited the demands of the story. For thematic reasons, Ilmatar had to be a world like Europa, with a shell of ice forever sealing off its inhabitants from the larger universe. Once I made that decision, the rest was more or less paint-by-numbers planetary science.

Creating the inhabitants was a question of fitting the beings to the story and to the planet. The Ilmatarans are suited to their environment: they sense the world via sonar, they don't use oxygen (which means they wear out easily). I wanted them to have a technological civilization, so that meant they had to have manipulating limbs. That in turn ruled out a fish-like being, and I felt that tentacles are a bit overdone in science fiction right now. So I built them on a crustacean model. That was partly just personal preference: the times I've been diving, the crustaceans are always the most interesting creatures to watch.

The culture of the Ilmatarans stems largely from their biology. They spawn, so sex is a trivial part of their lives. For Ilmatarans, the real emotional center of one's life is territory. Having a piece of property is what makes them "complete." Their culture reflects these elements: children are essentially wild animals, but the ones which survive to adulthood get educated and brought into the social system as "apprentices." An apprentice can aspire to inherit property or learn a trade.

Their laws are all about property, and about protecting the property owners (because over a very long history, the societies which didn't do that eventually collapsed into destructive all-against-all conflict). Ilmataran property owners are sovereign on their own territory—my hero Broadtail is convicted of murder when it is proved that his victim was killed beyond the boundary of Broadtail's property. Had it been within the boundary, the law would not touch him. I don't think this is an ideal system, particularly for humans, but it's one which works for at least one population of Ilmatarans.

Ilmataran technology was the result of a lot of thinking about what they could and could not build. They can grind and chip stone, they can weave and knit fibers, they can make rope, they can shape bone and material similar to wood. But they can't work metals, they can't make glass or pottery, their knowledge of chemistry will be minimal, and they are physically unable to study optics or astronomy. Since their world is lightless, they have little conception of measured time.

How about the Sholen?

For the Sholen, I had to design a society which would be very distinct from those of both the Ilmatarans and my human characters. I also needed to give them a strong reason for trying to interfere in the activities of other species across interstellar distances.

I decided that the Sholen are very passionate and sexual, with a society that sexualizes every relationship. What we would call sexual harassment they consider good leadership. Unfortunately, the result of their psychology has been a dreadful and tragic history. It seems logical that hypersexual beings would tend to overpopulate their world, leading to conflicts over scarce resources, environmental catastrophes, and so on. The poor Sholen have managed to suffer through every civilization-ending catastrophe humans have worried about. They've had nuclear wars, they've had a planetary environment collapse, they've seen it all.

The only way they can survive is to create a society based on consensus, where everybody has to agree about everything, and which limits their population to just a few hundred million. Unfortunately, this is quietly making the Sholen crazy. When they encounter humans, they project all their frustrations onto us. Because their own history is one of conquest and genocide and self-inflicted disasters on a scale that dwarfs anything we've managed, they assume the worst about us, and impose strict rules to protect the rest of the universe from humans. Things go downhill from there.

Did I stack the deck? Of course I did. I wanted conflict, after all, so I designed the Sholen to come into conflict with humans.

How different, if at all, was your approach to this novel than your approach to short fiction?

I had to learn a lot about writing longer works. A short story or even a novella is still small enough for me to hold in my mind. I can remember all the characters, the order of events, the world background and all the rest. For a novel that's impossible. *A Darkling Sea* has a relatively small cast compared to some books, but fourteen speaking parts and another dozen spear-carriers is simply too much for me to write off the top of my head. I had to keep careful notes, and I'm sure a few inconsistencies crept in despite that.

And in what ways was your work in tabletop games a help or hindrance?

It helped in a practical sense: I knew I could write 100,000-word projects (though I discovered writing fiction takes longer than game writing). It gave me the chance to hone my craft, as they say, and get paid for it. And as I mentioned, I got to do all my science research in the course of writing science fiction roleplaying games.

Running games for my friends also taught me how to narrate physical action. For most of my gamemastering career I never made much use of miniatures or a mapboard (because I'm too cheap to invest in a lot of lead figures and too klutzy to paint them). So I have become at least competent at describing a situation so that people can understand what's going on and what options they have. That turns out to be a useful skill when writing fiction.

However, I must confess roleplaying games have given me some bad storytelling habits as well. In most fiction, the protagonist struggles against adversity, his problems pile up, and we worry about how he's going to overcome his antagonists until the final struggle. Sometimes the worry is whether the protagonist can actually defeat his enemies, other times it's whether he will make the right moral choices and take the right actions. Either way, though, the bulk of most stories involve things getting steadily worse for the heroes.

Roleplaying games have a very different structure. In a typical game, the heroes encounter and overcome minor challenges, then greater ones, and each obstacle lets them gain the resources or knowledge to tackle the next ones, until they're finally ready to battle the main enemy. In other words, roleplaying games are about characters steadily improving. That's very different from fiction, and tends to drain away tension rather than ramping it up.

I had to keep reminding myself to make things worse for the heroes rather than better. If *A Darkling Sea* seems episodic, I think one can blame my roleplaying background.

What's at the heart of the book for you?

Those are two different questions. For me it's about whether it's a good thing for humans to gain knowledge. Knowledge means power, and power corrupts. But if we don't go out to learn about the Universe, then species like the Ilmatarans will live and ultimately go extinct without ever getting beyond their circumscribed world. (Yes, as I admitted above, I stacked the deck in order to make the issue as plain and starkly-defined as I could.) So for me, the heart of the book is the moment when Alicia shows Rob and Tizhos a colony of phosphorescent organisms in Ilmatar's ocean: something that nothing had ever seen before that moment.

How about for the characters?

For my characters, the heart of the story is quite different. Rob gains maturity, going from being a feckless overgrown adolescent to a hero capable of making tough choices. Broadtail loses his territory and status on Ilmatar but ultimately gains the entire Universe. And Tizhos has to break out of her consensus-based society to do the right thing.

Is there a character that you connect with *differently* than the others? One that's special? One that repulses you?

I poured a lot of my own worst qualities into Irona, the Sholen commander who leads them into disaster. Irona thinks he's a lot smarter and more virtuous than he really is. He's arrogant and vindictive and assumes the worst about others. And yet I kind of enjoyed writing his scenes, just because it's always fun to depict a really horrible person.

I think it's obvious that my favorite character in the book is Broadtail. He has a lot of qualities I wish I had. He can thrive and prosper within his society, and get along outside it. He's a scientist, an engineer, a farmer, an explorer, and a warrior.

What do you enjoy about writing fiction?

I suppose I could talk about the practical advantages—I work when and where I choose, I'm flexible and independent, I get to meet interesting people. But all those things are equally true of being a bank robber, and bank robbery pays better.

The part of writing I enjoy the most is when I get to feel clever: the times when the work really flows, and I know that what I'm writing is good. I expect that's what the ancients were thinking of when they invoked the Muse. Bank robbers probably never get that feeling. It doesn't happen very often, just often enough to keep me hooked and coming back for more.

ABOUT THE AUTHOR

Jeremy L. C. Jones is a freelance writer, editor, and teacher. He is the Staff Interviewer for *Clarkesworld Magazine* and a frequent contributor to *Kobold Quarterly* and *Booklifenow.com*. He teaches at Wofford College and Montessori Academy in Spartanburg, SC. He is also the director of Shared Worlds, a creative writing and world-building camp for teenagers that he and Jeff VanderMeer designed in 2006. Jones lives in Upstate South Carolina with his wife, daughter, and flying poodle.

Another Word:
The Words We Carry
JASON HELLER

When I was a kid, I carried around universes in a cardboard box.

My universes were heavy. But I was lucky. They all fit inside that box, even if their numbers kept expanding.

My universes were small. Like a certain famous British police box, they were bigger on the inside than on the outside. Way bigger. In fact, they were limited only by the imaginations of their creators.

My universes were books. I carried them around in a cardboard box because, when I was a kid, my family and I were always trying to keep one step ahead of an angry landlord, or an eviction notice, or simply, the street.

I grew up poor, and I grew up loving fantasy and science fiction. This shouldn't seem remarkable, yet it is. Most of the kids I knew who liked SFF were well-off—comfortably middle-class at the very worst. Meanwhile, most of the kids who came from my side of the tracks did everything they could to avoid the taint of geekery. Being a geek meant being weak, and when you're poor, being tough—or feigning toughness—is one of the first survival strategies you learn.

When it came to being tough, I was a failure. The best I could muster was aloofness. Then again, it's easy being alone when you *love* being alone—especially alone with a book. Or a whole box of them.

Reading SFF didn't curb my loneliness. Nor was it an escape. It's easy to paint SFF, and its fans, as escapism addicts. I grew up around real addicts. It's not the same. When I first read my uncle's dusty copy of Stephen R. Donaldson's brutal, morally murky *Lord Foul's Bane* at the age of eleven, I didn't escape my situation any more than the book's leprous antihero, Thomas Covenant, escaped his when he crossed over from modern-day Earth to the fantastic realm known as the Land. By the age of eleven, I'd already witnessed plenty of horrible things in real life, from nervous breakdowns to drunken destruction to domestic violence. *Lord Foul's Bane* only reminded me of them—and of the alienation, confusion, and rage that often come when kids, precocious or otherwise, are trapped in poverty.

Not all the books I read fueled that darkness. For every *Lord Foul's Bane* in my cardboard box there was a disintegrating, secondhand copy of Dragonriders of Pern. *Pern* isn't bright and happy—Anne McCaffrey was never strictly that—but compared to Donaldson, her work is more balanced and open to the notion of heroism. Again, though, there is no escapism.

Lessa, the heroine of *Dragonflight*, is caught in a caste system. Born noble, she's orphaned then forced to disguise herself as a menial drudge. As clichéd as that trope seems now, it captivated me. I wasn't a noble, but I could relate. Growing up in an unstable, alcoholic family that struggled to stay clothed, sheltered, and fed, I knew how subtly yet insidiously people could be treated according to where they fell in the economic hierarchy.

Looking back, it doesn't surprise me that I grew more intrigued by the Holdless, the lowest class on Pern, than I was by the dragonriding Weyrfolk. Lessa was an excellent character, but why did she have to be a royal reclaiming her birthright? Why couldn't she have been *born* a drudge? Why couldn't she be someone who fought her way upward without that inner assurance of entitlement?

There has been a call lately for more poor protagonists in SFF. I couldn't agree more. But it's just as much a matter of quality as quantity. Even with the unlimited scope and imaginative prerogative at the fingertips of the SFF writer, one outlandish concept still eludes most of them: that poor people might possibly see themselves, and reality, differently than those who have never gone homeless or hungry—and that such an outlook might lead to an entirely different kind of heroism.

Some have done so beautifully. Nalo Hopkinson's *Brown Girl in the Ring* immediately springs to mind, as does Nick Mamatas's latest novel *Love Is the Law*. Each acknowledges and addresses poverty in a way that's both integral to the story and unique to the author's voice. Neither panders. Neither excludes.

It's not that SFF isn't rife with poor protagonists. Woebegone serfs and dystopian proles litter the genre-scape, and the heroes among them are often the ones who feel contempt for their poorness. The problem lies in many authors' inability or unwillingness to portray their poor protagonists as anything other than middle-class people—with middle-class views of self and society—who simply wear tattered clothes and have a chip on their shoulders.

Oh, that chip. As a kid, I was angry. There were times that I went hungry. There were also times that my family was homeless—and if it weren't for the kindness of near strangers, we might not have made it. When you're a kid, and this is all you've ever known, you're not driven by ambition or redemption or revenge or any other kind of dramatic agency. You're driven by survival, except for the times when even survival seems like a luxury that maybe you don't even really deserve. But for every flash of anger and envy that I felt, I was gripped by other things. Fear. Excitement. Curiosity. Pensiveness. Desperation. Determination. Even, at the worst of times, a perverse sense of self-sabotage.

These are the kinds of conflicts, both internal and external, that I still crave to see more in SFF. It isn't an issue of economic justice, although I'd be lying if I said I wasn't deeply concerned about that. It's an issue of richness—the kind that has nothing to do with riches. Some positive steps have taken, like the new grant being launched by the Speculative Literary Foundation to catalyze diversity within the ranks of upcoming SFF writers. It's a start. More writers from disadvantaged backgrounds should be encouraged to write SFF. And when they do, they should be encouraged to write from that experience rather than expected to act like Lessa in reverse—a poor kid hewing to middle-class sensibilities for the sake of a genre that, on the whole, does not return the favor.

I'll never fully realize just how much all those books in my cardboard box helped me cope. They kept a poor, hungry, lonely kid occupied. And focused. And ever questioning. I can only guess what those books would have accomplished if people like me had actually *been* in them.

When I wish for more economic diversity in SFF, I'm not concerned about the health of genre fiction as a whole. I'm selfish like that. I want more of those books for *me*. More precisely, I want the younger versions of me to be able to go to a library sale, a secondhand bookstore, or a generous uncle and find more SFF books that understand what it means to be poor. Books that say there's no shame in growing up poor. Books that show how SFF has the ability, as no other literature does, of illuminating the human condition of being poor—the good and the bad.

I will always carry that box of books around with me. Not literally, of course. My bookshelves are now overflowing, if no less dusty. Thankfully I've managed to get to a point where I almost always know where my next meal is coming from and where I'll be laying my head that night. But I still carry around that same sense of wonder, and that same sense of frustration, that I did when I was a kid.

My universes were heavy. My universes were small. My universes were books. And they still are. Here's hoping they never stop growing.

ABOUT THE AUTHOR

Jason Heller is a former nonfiction editor of *Clarkesworld*; as part of the magazine's 2012 editorial team, he received a Hugo Award. He is also the author of the alternate history novel *Taft 2012* (Quirk Books) and a Senior Writer for *The Onion*'s pop-culture site, *The A.V. Club*. His short fiction has appeared in *Apex Magazine, Sybil's Garage,* and others, and his genre-related reviews and essays have been published in *Weird Tales, NPR.org, Tor.com,* and Ann and Jeff VanderMeer's *The Time Traveller's Almanac*. A graduate of the Odyssey Writing Workshop in 2009, he also teaches science fiction and fantasy at Lighthouse Writers Workshop. He lives in Denver with this wife Angela; between the two of them, they could build a house out of books. Maybe they already have.

Editor's Desk:
Reader's Poll Results
and Other Award News

NEIL CLARKE

Our 2013 Reader's Poll closed last month and I've been patiently await-
ing the opportunity to share the results with you. With no further ado,
I present this year's winners:

Cover Art

First Place:
"Silent Oracle"
by Matt Dixon

Second Place:
"Rainforest God"
by David Melvin

Third Place:
"Lost in Space"
by Piotr Foksowicz

Note: Matt took first place this year by a healthy margin, but over the month, five different works held the number two spot at least once.

Fiction

First Place: "The Urashima Effect" by E. Lily Yu
Second Place: "Effigy Nights" by Yoon Ha Lee
Third Place: "Silent Bridge, Pale Cascade" by Benjanun Sriduangkaew
Fourth Place: "The Promise of Space" by James Patrick Kelly
Fifth Place: "Cry of the Kharchal" by Vandana Singh

Note: The top five stories were a total of ten points apart, with the gap between first and second being the only place where there was more than a three point difference.

Other Awards and Recognition

Locus Magazine released their recommended reading list and it included the following *Clarkesworld* stories:

"Soulcatcher" by James Patrick Kelly
"The Promise of Space" by James Patrick Kelly
"Effigy Nights" by Yoon Ha Lee
"Mystic Falls" by Robert Reed
"Cry of the Kharchal" by Vandana Singh
"No Portraits on the Sky" by Kali Wallace

The annual Locus Poll is now open to everyone. You can participate at:

www.locusmag.com/Magazine/2014/PollAndSurvey.html

Hugo Award nominations are open until the end of this month. Unlike prior years, *Clarkesworld* is *not* eligible for the Hugo Award for Best Semiprozine. I encourage you to check out semiprozine.org for a list of many eligible magazines you can nominate. Of course, our stories and editors are also eligible in the appropriate categories. (See: neil-clarke.com/2014-awards-eligibility-hugo-nebula/ for a handy by-category list.)

I'd like to take this opportunity to thank our subscribers and everyone else that has supported us financially last year. Becoming ineligible for the Semiprozine Hugo is a milestone for us. It means that with your help we're moving towards our goal of becoming a full-time business. With that comes the time and resources to maintain and improve on what we can offer. We still have many milestones to go—for example, we're still non-professional in the eyes of the World Fantasy Award—but your support provides the confidence we need to believe we can get there.

Thank you!

ABOUT THE AUTHOR

Neil Clarke is the editor of *Clarkesworld Magazine,* owner of Wyrm Publishing and a two-time Hugo Nominee for Best Editor (short form). He currently lives in NJ with his wife and two children.

About the Artist
MATT DIXON

Matt Dixon is a freelance illustrator and concept artist from the UK. Digital art first captured his imagination when he began to assemble images from ASCII characters on a Commodore VIC-20 way back in 1980. Happily, things have moved along a little and Adobe Photoshop allows him to achieve slightly more sophisticated results these days.

His long association with the games industry began when he first contributed art to a video game in 1988. He was employed by one of the UK's largest independent games developers for more than a decade, initially as a production artist, then as an art lead. During this time he was privileged to be involved with numerous high profile game and movie licenses, including Harry Potter, Crash Bandicoot, Spyro the Dragon and Pirates of the Caribbean.

WEBSITE

www.mattdixon.co.uk